MEET THE FORTUNES!

Fortune of the Month: Stacey Fortune Jones

Age: 24

Vital Statistics: Blond hair, green eyes, stretch marks (sigh)

Claim to Fame: Raising bubbly baby girl all on her own

Romantic Prospects: None, or so she thinks. Romance and diapers just don't mix.

"I'm sure you've heard all the rumors. Folks are saying that Colton is interested in me. Colton Foster? Don't be ridiculous! He's known me since I was born! He's seen me with skinned knees and braces and all sorts of teenage awkwardness. And I just gave birth six months ago. Sexy, huh?

"The only trouble is, I've started having these, uh, feelings for *him.* And I have no idea what to do about them. It's so inappropriate—not to mention embarrassing! And I have a sinking suspicion that— yikes!—Colton has *figured it o*

Dear Reader,

I'm crazy for the Horseback Hollow Fortunes! I love my parents, but after spending some time with these new Fortunes, I also want to be an honorary member of the Fortune family. Jeanne Marie Fortune Jones is such a nurturing mama, and the rest of this group of Fortunes know the true meaning of love and family...or are learning the true meaning of love. They're good people. They step up and help each other and their community. Doesn't that sound like a family you would like to have?

In my book, Stacey Fortune Jones has had some struggles during the past year and a half. Her fiancé dumped her via a note after he learned she was pregnant, and Stacey is now a single mom temporarily living with her parents while she gets back on her feet. Now that she has a baby daughter, Piper, her focus is motherhood and helping around her parents' house. Stacey tries not to think about the fact that she may never find a man who will love her and her daughter.

But could Mr. Forever live only five minutes away? Colton Foster, whose ranch borders Stacey's parents', has always viewed Stacey as a little sister. After all, Stacey and his younger sister are best friends. When he sees Stacey at a New Year's Eve wedding celebration, she seems more grown-up, more womanly. Colton can't get the new Stacey out of his mind, but the tough rancher finds her baby daughter "scary." Complications abound. Can these two forever friends become forever lovers?

I hope you'll enjoy this chance to join the Horseback Hollow Fortune family. There are five more exciting stories by fabulous authors to come!

Happy reading,

Leanne Banks

Happy New Year, Baby Fortune!

Leanne Banks

HARLEQUIN SPECIAL EDITION®

Special thanks and acknowledgment are given to Leanne Banks for her contribution to The Fortunes of Texas: Welcome to Horseback Hollow continuity.

Recycling programs
for this product may
not exist in your area.

ISBN-13: 978-0-373-65787-2

HAPPY NEW YEAR, BABY FORTUNE!

Printed in U.S.A.

Books by Leanne Banks

Harlequin Special Edition

Silhouette Special Edition

Silhouette Desire

Other titles by Leanne Banks
available in ebook format.

LEANNE BANKS

is a *New York Times* and *USA TODAY* bestselling author who is surprised every time she realizes how many books she has written. Leanne loves chocolate, the beach and new adventures. To name a few, Leanne has ridden an elephant, stood on an ostrich egg (no, it didn't break), gone parasailing and indoor skydiving. Leanne loves writing romance, because she believes in the power and magic of love. She lives in Virginia with her family and a four-and-a-half-pound Pomeranian named Bijou. Visit her website, www.leannebanks.com.

Chapter One

Stacey Fortune Jones was sure she had the cutest date at the New Year's Eve wedding reception for her cousin Sawyer Fortune and his bride, Laurel Redmond.

"Your baby is just gorgeous," Sherry James, one of her neighbors, said as she patted Stacey's six-month-old daughter's arm. "She has the best smile."

"Thank you," Stacey said. Clothed in a red velvet dress with a lace headband, white tights and red shoes, her little Piper was a true head turner. Stacey had enjoyed getting Piper ready for her first big night out, and it seemed her daughter was having fun. Her big green gaze took in all the sights and sounds of the celebration, and she smiled easily with everyone who approached. "She's a sweet baby now that she's gotten through her colic."

Sherry made a sympathetic clucking noise. "Colic can be hard on both the baby and the parents."

Stacey gave a vague nod. "So true," she said. In Stacey's case, there was no need for the plural. There was no dad to help. He'd abandoned Stacey before Piper had even been born. Thank goodness her parents had let her move back in with them.

"Well, you've obviously done a great job with her. She's the belle of the ball tonight," Sherry said.

"Thank you," Stacey said again.

"Oh, my husband's calling me," Sherry said. "You take care, now."

Jiggling her daughter Piper on her hip, Stacey headed for an empty seat at a table to give her feet a rest. Looking around, she couldn't believe that an airplane hangar could be transformed into such a beautiful reception site. Miles of tulle and lights decorated the space, and buffet tables groaned with delicious food. The sounds of a great band and happy voices echoed throughout the building. The guests, dressed in their finest, added to a celebratory mood. This wedding was the event of the season for the citizens of the small town of Horseback Hollow, Texas. People would be talking about it for years to come.

Although some might consider the choice of an airplane hangar a strange place to hold a wedding, it suited the groom and bride, since this was where the two were running a flight school together. No one had thought Sawyer or Laurel would ever settle down, let alone with each other. But the two stubborn yet free-spirited people had come to the conclusion that they were perfect for each other.

Stacey watched the newly married couple dance together and couldn't help thinking about the wedding she had been planning with her ex, Joe. Sometimes she wondered if she had ever really known Joe at all, or if she had been in love with an illusion of the man she'd wanted him to be. Now she didn't know if she'd ever find the love she saw on the faces of the bride and groom. Even though the hangar was filled with family and friends, and her little Piper was in her arms, Stacey suddenly felt alone.

"Hey," a male voice said. "How's it going?"

Stacey blinked to find her longtime neighbor, Colton Foster, sitting beside her. She gave herself a mental shake and tried to pull herself out of her blue moment. Colton's sister, Rachel, was Stacey's best friend; but Stacey had been overwhelmed with taking care of Piper, so she hadn't seen him except in passing since the baby had been born.

She'd known the Foster family forever. Colton had graduated several years earlier from the same high school she'd attended. He'd always been quiet and hardworking. He was the firstborn and only son of the Fosters and had taken his responsibilities seriously.

Tonight he wore a dark suit along with a Stetson, but he usually dressed his tall, athletic body in jeans and work boots. He had brown eyes that seemed to see beneath the surface, brown wavy hair and a strong jaw. Stacey knew of several women who'd had crushes on him, but to Stacey, he would always be Rachel's older brother.

"Great," she said. "I'm doing great. Piper doesn't have colic anymore, so I've actually gotten a few nights of sleep. My parents adore her. My brothers and sister adore her. She's healthy and happy. Life couldn't be better," she insisted, willing herself to believe it.

Stacey searched Colton's face. She couldn't help wondering if he'd heard anything from Joe since he and her ex had been good friends. Colton had even been asked to be one of the groomsmen for Stacey and Joe's wedding. The question was on the tip of her tongue, but she swallowed it without asking. Did she really want to know? It wasn't as if she wanted him back. Still, Piper deserved to know her father, she thought. Stacey's stomach twisted as she met the gaze of her quiet neighbor. Maybe Stacey just wanted to hear that Joe was miserable without her.

The silence between them stretched. "She's a cute baby," Colton finally said.

Stacey smiled at her daughter. "Yes, she is. Someone even called her the belle of the ball," she said. "How are things with you?"

"Same as always," he said with a shrug. "Working a lot of hours to keep the ranch going."

Stacey searched for something else to say. The

gap in conversation between her and Colton felt so awkward. She couldn't remember ever feeling this uncomfortable with him. "I haven't gotten out very much since Piper was born, so it's been a while since I've seen a lot of people or been to such a big party."

He nodded. "Yeah. Rachel tells me she drops by your house every now and then. She's been keeping us updated on how you're doing."

"Rachel has always been a good friend. I don't know what I would have done without her when—" Stacey broke off, determined not to mention Joe's name aloud. She cleared her throat and decided to change the direction of the conversation. "Well, I'm glad you're doing well," she said, almost wishing he would leave. Maybe then she wouldn't feel so awkward.

Another silence stretched between them, and Stacey almost decided to leave despite the fact that Piper was half-asleep in her arms.

"It's a new year," Colton finally said. "A new year is always a good time for a fresh start. Are you planning to go back to work soon?"

Stacey sighed. "I'm not sure what to do now. I loved my job. I was a nurse at the hospital in Lubbock, but the idea of leaving Piper just tears me up. Even though my mother would babysit for me, it wouldn't be fair. My mother is busy enough without taking on the full care of a baby. Plus, I hate the idea of being so far away if Piper should need me."

"Is there anywhere else closer you could work?" he asked.

"I've thought about that, but as you know, the employment opportunities here in Horseback Hollow aren't great. There's no hospital here. It's frustrating because I don't want to be dependent on my parents. At the same time, I'm Piper's one and only parent, and I'm determined that she gets all the love she needs and deserves."

Colton studied Stacey for a long moment and realized that something about his younger sister's friend had changed. She used to be so happy and carefree. Now it seemed as if there was a shadow clouding the sunny optimism she'd always exhibited. He couldn't help feeling a hard stab of guilt. He wondered if the conversation he'd had with Joe over a year ago had influenced the man to propose to Stacey. Maybe he shouldn't have warned Joe that he might lose Stacey to someone else if he didn't put a ring on her finger. If they hadn't gotten engaged, maybe she wouldn't have gotten pregnant and Joe wouldn't have left her. After Joe had left Stacey pregnant with his child, Colton's opinion of his friend had plummeted. Now he wondered if Joe had just felt possessive about Stacey. He obviously hadn't loved her the way she deserved to be loved. Colton had always known Joe's home life hadn't been the best when he was growing up, but in Colton's mind, that was no excuse for how Joe had treated Stacey.

More than Stacey's outlook had changed, Colton noticed. She just seemed more grown-up. His gaze dipped to her body, and he couldn't help noticing she was curvier than she used to be. She'd filled out in all the right places. He glanced at her face and saw that her eyes seemed to contain a newfound knowledge.

Stacey had become a woman, he concluded. She was no longer the young girl who'd giggled constantly with his younger sister Rachel. He watched her lift a glass to her lips and take a sip of champagne, then slide her tongue over her lips.

The motion made his gut clench in an odd way. He wondered how her lips would feel against his. He wondered how her body would feel....

Shocked at the direction his mind was headed, Colton reined in his thoughts. This was *Stacey,* for Pete's sake. Not some random girl at a bar. He cleared his throat.

Stacey glanced around the room. "There are a *lot* of Fortunes. I'm still trying to keep all the names straight."

"That's for sure. Do you know all of them?" he asked.

Stacey shot him a sideways glance. "I've been introduced to all of them. I'm trying my best to remember their names. Between my mother, her brother James and her sister, Josephine, they have thirteen children."

Colton gave a low whistle. "That's a lot."

"And that doesn't include the wives. Just about

all of James Fortune's children have gotten married within the last year," she said.

"I'm curious. What made all of you take on the Fortune name?"

She shrugged. "We did it for Mom. I know it sounds weird, but for Mama, finding her birth family has been a big deal. Even though her adoptive parents loved and adored her, there were things about her past that seemed a big mystery because she knew she was adopted. I think that meeting her brother James and her sister, Josephine, makes her feel more complete. For my mom, taking on the Fortune name is a symbolic way of declaring her connection to the Fortune family. Most of us have added the Fortune name out of respect to her. My brother Liam is holding out, though."

"How does your father feel about it?"

"That's a good question," she said. "My father is very stoic. He hasn't said anything aloud, and he has loved my mother pretty much since the dawn of time, but I have a feeling he may not like the name change. I'm not sure he would ever say it, because he's supportive of my mom. He would always have her back, but I wouldn't blame him if this pinched his ego a little bit."

"Speaking of your Mama Jeanne," Colton said. "She's coming this way."

Stacey smiled. "Betcha she wants to show off her grandbaby. Watch and see."

Stacey's mother wore her snowy white hair on

the back of her head, and she sported a nice but not fancy dress. Jeanne Marie Fortune Jones was one of the most welcoming women Colton had ever met. Everyone in Horseback Hollow loved the nurturing woman. Jeanne extended her arms as she got close to Stacey and the baby. "Give me that little peanut," Mrs. Jones said. "It's time for me to give you a little break."

"She's been fine," Stacey said, handing over the baby to her mother. "I think she is half-asleep."

"Already? At her first party?" Mrs. Jones adjusted Piper's headband. "I need to introduce her to a few people before she totally zonks out." Mrs. Jones glanced at Colton. "Good to see you and your family here tonight. We're glad you could make it," she said.

"Wouldn't miss it," he said. "It was nice of you to make sure we were invited."

"Well, of course you're invited. You're like family to us. What do you think of little Piper here?" she asked, beaming with pride.

"She's a pretty little thing," Colton said, although babies made him a little uneasy. Seemed as if they could start screaming like wild banshees with no cause or warning.

"That she is," Mrs. Jones said. "I just want to make sure James and Josephine get to see her. You take a little break, Stacey."

Stacey nodded and smiled as her mother left. "Told you she wanted to show her off."

Colton glanced at Stacey's mother as she joined her Fortune siblings at a table and bounced the baby on her knee. The other woman, Josephine, smiled at the baby and jiggled the baby's hand.

Stacey smiled as she looked at her mother and her aunt and uncle. They were still learning about each other, but they were growing in love for each other, too.

"So, how does it feel to be a Fortune?" Colton asked.

"I don't know," Stacey said. "It may take some time to figure it out."

"Well, it must be nice not to have to worry about money anymore," he said.

Stacey shook her head and gave a short chuckle. "You must not have heard. My mother gave back the Fortune money. She didn't feel right about accepting it."

"Whoa," Colton said.

Stacey nodded. "Her brother James wanted to give her a lot of money. But she felt that money rightfully should go to his children. Mama doesn't want her relationship with James and the rest of the Fortunes tainted by her taking money from him."

Colton shook his head. "Your mama is an amazing woman. That was an honorable thing to do."

"I think so, too, but not everyone agrees with her decision," Stacey said. "For Mama's sake, I hope everything will turn out okay."

At that moment, Jeanne Fortune Jones was in heaven. Sharing her grandbaby with her newly discovered brother and sister, with family all around, Jeanne felt complete. Jeanne had always known she was adopted. Her parents had loved her as if they'd given birth to her, perhaps more. Yet even with all that love and adoration, something had been missing. Now she knew what it was—her brother and sister. Joined together in the womb as triplets, separated for most of their lives, the three of them were back together again. To Jeanne, it all seemed a beautiful circle of life.

Her often-stern-faced brother James cleared his throat. "Jeanne, I still wish you would accept the money I tried to give you earlier. It feels wrong. Won't you reconsider?"

Jeanne immediately shook her head. Her conviction was clear as crystal on this matter. Jeanne knew that James's children had turned their backs on him because they'd misunderstood James's attempted generosity toward Jeanne. Now, after months of an angry, silent divide, James and his family were being reunited. "Absolutely not. I refuse to be the cause of a rift between you and your children. Besides, you earned that money. I didn't have anything to do with it."

James sighed. "But I feel guilty that I have so much and you have so little."

Jeanne shook her head and smiled as she looked down at her sweet granddaughter. "I've been around long enough to know that there are all kinds of riches. I have a wonderful husband, loving children and this beautiful grandchild. And now I have the two of you. My life couldn't be happier. I feel like I'm the lucky one."

"Do the rest of your family members feel that way?" James asked doubtfully.

Jeanne thought of her son Christopher and his resentment. Chris just had some growing up to do. He would realize what was truly important in due time. At least, she hoped he would. "Mostly," she said. "Look at how most of my kids have accepted the Fortune name. They know I would do anything for them, and they would do anything for me."

Jeanne noticed her sister seemed quieter than usual. "Are you okay, Josephine? Is this party too much for you?"

Josephine shook her head. "No. It's a grand party. You Texans know how to pull out all the stops," she said in her lovely British accent.

Jeanne Marie studied her refined sister in her luxury designer clothing. Who would have ever thought that she, Jeanne Jones, could be related to a woman who had married into the British royal family?

The thought made her laugh. She and James and Josephine had been joined in the womb. That was the ultimate equality. But more important than that, Jeanne knew herself, her heart and her family. She was beyond happy with her life. She sensed, however, that James and Josephine might not be so happy with theirs, but she hoped she was wrong....

"All of my children are single. I hope they will

find love someday," Josephine murmured under her breath.

"Of course they will," Jeanne said, patting her sister's hand. "It just takes some time."

Josephine looked at Jeanne with a soft gaze. "I'm so glad we found each other."

Jeanne squeezed her sister's hand. "I am, too."

From across the room, Stacey enjoyed watching her mother with her siblings, but then she caught sight of her brother Chris striding toward her. His face looked like a thundercloud. "Uh-oh."

"I need to talk to you for a moment," Chris said, and gave Colton a short nod. "Excuse us."

Stacey lifted her lips in a smile that she suspected resembled more of a wince. "Excuse me," she said, and followed Christopher to a semiquiet corner of the airplane hangar.

"Do you see how chummy Mama Jeanne is being with James and Josephine? It makes me sick to my stomach to see her being so nice to them," he said.

"Well, of course she's being nice to them. She's thrilled she finally found out that she has brothers and a sister. You know Mama has always wondered about her birth family."

"That's not the point," Christopher said. "I don't understand how she is all right with the fact that her brothers James and John grew up with boatloads of money. And her sister, Josephine, was married to British royalty, for Pete's sake. It's not fair that they're so wealthy and she's had to watch every dime."

Chris had always been ambitious, pretty much since birth. The status quo wasn't going to be enough for him. Stacey had long known he wanted more for himself and the whole family. Chris and their father, Deke, had rubbed each other wrong on this subject on more than one occasion.

Stacey hated to see her brother so upset when she knew her mother was thrilled with the recent discovery of her siblings. "Mama's life hasn't been so bad. She has all of us kids and a great husband. They both have good health and would support each other through thick and thin." She couldn't help thinking about how Joe had left her high and dry once he'd learned she was pregnant. Her father wouldn't dream of doing anything like that to her mother.

Chris's eye twitched, and Stacey could tell he wasn't the least bit appeased. "It's still not fair. Tell the truth. Wouldn't it be nice if we didn't have to worry about money? Think about Piper. Wouldn't you like to know she would have everything she needs?"

"Piper will have everything she needs. Her life may not be filled with luxury, but she will get what she needs," Stacey insisted, feeling defensive because she wasn't making any money right now.

"Yeah, but you gotta admit things could be easier," he said.

Stacey sighed. "They could be," she admitted,

but shook her head. "But I can't let myself go there. I'm going to have to make my own way. There's no fairy tale happening for me."

"I'm not asking for a fairy tale. I'm just thinking Mom should at least get a piece of the pie," he said. "Seems to me that Mom's new brother and sister are greedy and selfish."

"It's not James Fortune's fault that we aren't getting any Fortune money. James gave her money, and Mama *chose* to give the money back. James may be a little stiff, but he seems nice enough. He really didn't even have to offer the money to Mama in the first place, but he did. I bet if any of us really needed financial help that he would be glad to help."

Chris tilted his head to one side in a thoughtful way, and Stacey could practically see the wheels turning in his mind. "You may have a point. I think I'll have a word with *Uncle* James."

Stacey opened her mouth to tell him to think it over before he approached their new relative, but he was gone before she could say a word. Stacey twisted her fingers together. She wished Chris wouldn't get so worked up about this, but she feared her discussion with him hadn't helped one bit.

Sighing, she glanced away and caught sight of the bride and groom, Laurel and Sawyer, snuggling in a corner, feeding each other bites of wedding cake. The sight was so romantic. She could tell by the expressions on their faces that they clearly adored each other. Her heart twisted. She wondered if anyone would ever look at her that way.

Stacey gave herself a hard mental shake and reminded herself that her priority was Piper now. She surveyed the room, looking for her baby, and saw that her new aunt Josephine was holding Piper in her arms. Mama Jeanne was sitting right beside her. Stacey knew her mother would guard the baby like a bear with its cub. Stacey told herself she had a lot to be grateful for with such a supportive family.

Feeling thirsty, she navigated her way through the crowd toward the fountain of punch and got a cup. She took several sips and glanced up. Her gaze met Colton's. He was looking at her with a strange expression on his face. She felt a little dip in her stomach. What was that? she wondered. Why was he looking at her that way? And why did her stomach feel funny? Maybe she'd better get a bite to eat.

She wandered to one of the food tables and nibbled on a few appetizers.

"Everything okay with Chris?" Colton asked from behind her.

She turned around and was grateful her stomach didn't do any more dipping. "I'm not sure. Chris has some things he needs to work out. I wish I could help him, but he can have a one-track mind sometimes. Unfortunately, I think this may be one of those times."

"You want me to talk to him?" he asked.

"He might listen to you more than he does me,

but I think this is something he's going to have to work out on his own," she said and rolled her eyes. "Brothers."

He chuckled and looked at the dance floor. "I'm not the best dancer in the world, but I can probably spin you around a few times without stepping on your feet. Do you want to dance?"

She blinked in surprise. Stacey couldn't remember the last time she'd danced except with Piper. His invitation made her feel almost like a real human being, more than a mother. She smiled. "I'd like that very much."

Stacey stepped into Colton's arms, and they danced a Western-style waltz to the romantic tune. Of course she would never have romantic feelings for Colton, but she couldn't help noticing his broad shoulders and how strong he felt. It was nice to be held, even if it was just as friends. Taking a deep breath, she caught the scent of his cologne and leather. Looking into his brown eyes, she thought she'd always liked the steadfast honesty in his gaze. Colton was Mr. Steady, all male and no nonsense. Looking closer, she observed, for the first time, though, that he had long eyelashes. She'd never noticed before. Maybe because she'd never been this close to him?

"What are you thinking?" he asked.

She felt a twinge of self-consciousness. "Nothing important."

"Then why are you staring at me? Do I have some food on my face?"

Her lips twitched, and she told herself to get over her self-consciousness. After all, this was Colton. He might as well be one of her brothers. "If you must know, Mr. Nosy, I was thinking that you have the longest eyelashes I've ever seen on a man. A lot of women would give their eyeteeth for your eyelashes."

Surprise flashed through his eyes, and he laughed. It was a strong, masculine, happy sound that made her smile. "That's a first."

"No one else has ever told you that?" she asked and narrowed her eyes in disbelief. Although Colton wasn't one to talk about his romantic life, and he certainly was no womanizer, she knew he'd spent time with more than a woman or two. "Can you honestly tell me no woman has ever complimented you on your long eyelashes?"

"Not that I can remember," he said, which sounded as if he was hedging to Stacey. He shrugged. "The ladies usually give me other kinds of compliments," he said in a low voice that bordered on sensual.

Surprise and something else rushed through Stacey. She had never thought of Colton in those terms, and she wasn't now, she told herself. "What kinds of compliments?" she couldn't resist asking.

"Oh, this and that."

Another nonanswer, she thought, her curiosity piqued.

The song drew to a close, and the bandleader

tapped on his microphone. "Ladies and gentlemen, we have less than a minute left to this year. It's time for the countdown."

A server delivered horns and noisemakers and confetti pops. Stacey absently accepted a noisemaker and confetti pop and looked around for her baby. "I wonder if Piper is still with Mama Jeanne," she murmured, then caught sight of her mother holding a noisemaker for the baby.

"…five…four…three…two…one," the bandleader said. "Happy New Year!"

Stacey met Colton's gaze while many couples kissed to welcome the New Year, and she felt a twist of self-consciousness. Maybe a hug would do.

Colton gave a shrug. "May as well join the crowd," he said, and lowered his head and kissed her just beside her lips. Closer to her mouth than her cheek, the sensation of the kiss sent a ripple of electricity throughout her body.

What in the world? she thought, staring up at him as he met her gaze.

"Happy New Year, Stacey."

Chapter Two

Colton couldn't get Stacey Fortune Jones off his mind.

Even now as he was taking inventory in one of the feed sheds with his dad, he wasn't paying full attention. He told himself it was because beneath Stacey's sunny smile, he sensed a deep sadness. That bothered him, especially since he wondered if he could have prevented it. He remembered the day he'd told his friend Joe, Stacey's ex, that Stacey was a special girl. If Joe didn't want to lose her, then he'd better put a ring on it. The very next day Joe had proposed, and Stacey had gone full speed ahead with the wedding plans. The result had been a disaster and Colton still blamed himself. If only he'd kept his mouth shut. He'd known Stacey was crazy about

Joe. Colton had thought Joe had just needed a little nudge. How wrong he'd been.

His father turned to him. "Did you input that last number I gave you?"

Colton bit the inside of his jaw. "Sorry. You mind repeating it?"

"What's wrong with you?" his father asked. "You seem as if you're a million miles away. Did you catch that virus that's going around?"

Colton shook his head, thinking the only virus he had caught was the guilt virus. He'd been fighting that one for a while now, and it had only gotten worse when he'd seen Stacey at the wedding. "No. I was just thinking about that extension course I'm taking and if we're going to want to spend the money on the improvements to the ranch that I've been learning about during my last lesson."

"Well, we've already got these e-tablet gizmos. Part of me likes that you're keeping us up to speed, but these e-tablets weren't cheap."

"Yes, I know," Colton said, his lips twitching in amusement. "You sure like playing solitaire on yours when you're not using it for work, don't you?"

His father shot him a mock glare, then made a sound somewhere between a cough and a chuckle. "All right, you've made your point. Let's get back to work, so you can take a break. You're acting like you need it."

"I don't—"

"Then what's the last number I gave you?" his father countered.

Colton frowned. "Okay, give me the number again," he said, but he sure didn't want a break. He needed to keep busy so he wouldn't be thinking about how he had contributed to ruining Stacey's life.

Despite his father's encouragement to take a break after doing inventory, Colton drove his truck out to check some fences that had been questionable in the past. Although January wasn't the busiest time for the ranch since the foals wouldn't come until spring, there was still plenty to do. Keeping the mamas healthy, safe and fed meant he had to stay on top of the condition of the fences and the pastures.

Colton checked several stretches of fence and only found one weak area. He made a note of it and returned to the family ranch. He'd been born and raised in the sprawling ranch house. After he'd turned twenty-five, they'd added an extra wing so that he could have some privacy. The fact that his room was farther from the center of the house usually worked for him, but there were times he just wanted his own place. Someday soon he would broach the subject with his father. Colton had a lot of money in the bank and in investments, so he could easily fund the purchase of a new home, but building Colton's home seemed like a matter of pride for Colton's father, Frank. All too aware of ranch finances, Colton didn't want to provide any extra strain. His father was still strong and healthy, but his back wasn't the best. Colton wanted to ease his burdens, not make them worse.

As he climbed the steps to the porch, he thought of Stacey again and made a decision. He was going to try to find a way to help bring back her sunny disposition. There had to be a way. Passing by the den, he saw his sister Rachel watching a reality matchmaker show on television. Those kinds of shows drove him crazy. He couldn't understand why Rachel watched them. The couples never ended up staying together. Obviously he didn't understand the female psyche.

Colton shrugged. Maybe he should pick Rachel's brain. Not only was she female, but she was also Stacey's best friend. Perhaps she could give him a few ideas. He grabbed a glass of water from the kitchen, then returned to the den and sank onto a chair.

"How's it going?" he asked when Rachel couldn't seem to tear her attention from the television show.

"Pretty good," she said, glancing at him. "I'm taking a little break from making lesson plans for student teaching. How about you?"

"Good," he said. "It's quiet. No trouble. Have you heard anything about Dad's back?"

"Not lately," she said. "I wish he would go to the doctor. I don't see how he's going to get better if he doesn't try to do anything about it."

"I try to keep him from doing things that might hurt him, but I can't be by his side every minute," he said.

"True," she said. "He's lucky you're around as

much as you are." She shot him a playful smile. "Colton, the saint."

"Yeah, right," he said in a dark voice. "Listen, I wanted to ask you something."

"What's that?" she asked, glancing back at the television. "Mom told me to tell you there's a potpie in the fridge if you want to heat it up for dinner."

"I'm not asking about dinner. I want to know what women want," he said.

She swiveled her head around to gape at him. "Well, that's a loaded question."

He lifted his shoulders. "Seems pretty straight-on to me. What do women want?"

Rachel laughed. "There's no one perfect answer. It depends on the woman." She looked at him with curiosity in her eyes. "Who do you have in mind?"

Colton resisted the urge to squirm under her inquisitive gaze. He'd rather die than admit he had Stacey on his mind. "Forget I said anything," he said and started to rise.

"Now, wait just a minute. You asked me a question. The least you can do is give me a chance to try to give you some suggestions." She looked at him suspiciously. "Although I can't help wondering who you're trying to please. And I don't have to tell you that nothing stays secret in Horseback Hollow for long."

"I know," he said.

Rachel sighed in frustration. "Well, there are the die-hard regulars," she said. "Roses and flowers."

Colton shook his head. "Nothing that obvious."

"Hmm," Rachel said. "The truth is that what most women want is a man who listens."

Colton frowned and shook his head. "That can't be it."

Rachel stared at him for a long moment. "I have an idea," she said, picking up her cell phone and dialing.

"What are you doing?" he asked, but his sister wasn't paying any attention to him.

"Stacey," Rachel said, sliding Colton a sly glance. "My brother needs a consultation. Can you come over?"

Colton nearly croaked. "Stacey?" he echoed.

Rachel nodded. "Great," she said into the phone. "See you in a few minutes." She disconnected the call and smiled at Colton. "This is great. You'll have advice from two women instead of just one."

Oh, Lord, what had he gotten himself into? "I think I'll heat up some of that potpie," Colton said, hatching an escape plan.

"Don't go too far. Stacey will be here soon," Rachel said, then shot him a crafty glance. "And don't take off for your bedroom. I know where to find you."

Colton stifled a groan. This was why he needed his own place. He was too accessible. Colton heated the potpie and returned to the den, telling himself he would set a mental time limit of fifteen minutes for the insanity about to ensue. He scarfed down as much food as possible during the next few moments.

A knock sounded at the door, but Stacey didn't wait for anyone to answer. She'd been bursting through that door as long as he could remember. "Hey, Rachel, I'm here," she called as she made her way to the den. Dressed in a winter-white coat, she carried her baby on her hip with ease. Piper wore a red coat and cap, and her cheeks were flushed with good health. She stared curiously around the room with her big, green eyes.

"Give me that sweet baby," Rachel said, rushing to reach for Piper.

Piper allowed herself to be taken from Stacey, but the baby watched to make sure her mama was in sight. Rachel unfastened the baby's coat and took off her cap.

Stacey shrugged out of her own coat and glanced from Rachel to Colton. "What's this about a consultation? Why on earth would Colton need a consultation from us?"

Rachel's face lit with mischief. "Colton asked me what women really want. We need to brainstorm Colton's love life."

Stacey looked at Colton in confusion. "I always thought Colton got along as well as he wanted to in that department. I've heard from a few girls who—" She cleared her throat. "Well, they seemed to like him just fine."

"Thank you, Stacey. I have gotten along just fine

in that department, despite my sister's opinion," he said in a dry voice.

Rachel jiggled the baby on her hip. "Well, this one must be different if you're asking *me* what women want," Rachel said.

Colton checked his watch. Thirteen minutes to go. This was going to feel like an eternity.

"Who is this girl?" Stacey asked, curiously gazing at Colton.

"He won't tell," Rachel answered for him.

Colton figured his sister was good for something.

"Well, what kind of woman is she? Country or city?" Stacey asked.

"If she's here, she's only one kind," Rachel said. "Country. We have no city to speak of."

"Hmm," Stacey said, and Colton again resisted the urge to squirm. "You could take her to dinner."

"Out of town," Rachel added. "People are so nosy here."

"Flowers would be good," Stacey said.

"He said flowers are too obvious," Rachel said.

Stacey frowned. "Too obvious?" she echoed.

"What if I just wanted to cheer her up?" Colton asked. "What if I don't necessarily want to date her?"

Rachel scowled. "Oh, that's a totally different matter. You don't want to be with her?"

Colton ground his teeth. "That's not the priority."

"So, you may want to be with her in the future?" Rachel asked.

"Let's deal with the present," he said in a grumbly voice.

"In that case—" Rachel said.

"Just visit her," Stacey said firmly. "And let her talk, maybe about what's been going on with her. Try and keep the conversation light. Nothing heavy."

"Small talk," Rachel said cheerfully.

Colton frowned. "What the hell is small talk besides weather?"

Both Stacey and Rachel laughed. "Nothing too deep," Rachel said. "You can even talk about clothing."

Colton scowled. "Clothing?" he echoed.

Stacey and Rachel exchanged an amused glance. "Work on it," Rachel said. "Read the paper. There may be something there you can chit-chat about."

"You could take her to get ice cream," Stacey said.

"In the winter?" Colton asked.

"I love ice cream any time of year," she confessed.

"If you really want to cheer up a woman, you could take a DVD of a chick flick and watch it with her," Rachel added.

Colton made a face. "If you say so," he said.

"Well, you asked," Rachel said with a bit of a testy tone. "Is this girl sick or just depressed? I know you said flowers are too obvious, but you could just happen to have some extra chocolates in your truck. Chocolate makes just about everything better."

"Except labor pains," Stacey said. "Chocolate doesn't help with labor pains."

Colton cleared his throat. He didn't like the direction this conversation was headed in. "I think I'm done with my dinner now."

"I'll take your plate," Rachel said. "You take Piper."

Colton pulled back.

Stacey shot him a look of surprise. "Oh, for goodness' sakes. You're not afraid of a baby, are you?"

"Of course I'm not afraid," he said, lying through his teeth. She was cute, but she was so *little*.

"Then, you can hold her," Rachel said, pushing Piper into his arms. "She's not radioactive."

Colton held the baby away from his body, staring into her face. She squirmed in his hands.

"You need to hold her closer," Stacey said. "She feels insecure in that position."

"I'm not gonna drop her," he said.

"I know that, but she doesn't," Stacey said.

He sat and gingerly set her on his lap, and she stopped wiggling.

Piper cooed at him, lifting her finger toward his face. She seemed to stare at his every feature. What amazing concentration she had. He inhaled and caught a whiff of sweet baby smell. Colton felt a strange sensation inside him, as if the baby was trying to communicate with him. She was a cute thing. He felt an odd protective feeling for the child even though Piper wasn't his. It was as if he was suddenly driven to keep her safe. At the same time, he was terrified she was going to start screaming any minute.

"You look so nervous, Colton. I can take her," Stacey said, lifting the baby from his arms.

Colton felt a huge sense of relief. At the same time, he wouldn't mind breathing in Piper's sweet scent again.

"So, did our advice help?" Stacey asked as she shifted Piper onto her hip.

Colton couldn't stop his gaze from flowing down her curvy body, then up again. A flash of what her nude body might look like slid through his brain. Colton gulped. Stacey—his sister's friend, the literal girl next door—was unbelievably sexy. Colton wondered if he was going insane.

"Isn't she sweet?" Stacey asked.

Colton lifted his head in a round nod. "Sweet," he said. *But frightening,* he thought, although he would never admit it in a million years. Colton was no baby expert, and he had no idea what to do with a tot like Piper. For that matter, he wasn't sure what to do with all the forbidden thoughts he was having about Stacey.

Later that night when Stacey had finally put Piper to sleep, she headed for her own bed after she'd washed her face and brushed her teeth. She couldn't shake the image of Colton holding Piper. The baby had taken to Colton almost immediately. He didn't know it, but Stacey did. Colton had looked wary about Piper, but the baby had clearly found him fascinating. She'd stared into his face as if she'd wanted to memorize every feature.

Stacey had found herself watching him more than she ever had in the past. Crazy, she told herself and closed her eyes and took several deep breaths. She counted backward from two hundred and finally fell asleep and into a vivid dream. Piper was crawling down the aisle of a chapel wearing her christening gown. Her sweet baby finally reached the altar, and Joe stood, with his back to Stacey.

"I do," Joe said.

Her heart pounding, Stacey tried to scream, but no sound came from her mouth. She felt utterly helpless.

"Joe," she whispered. "Joe…"

Stacey rushed toward the altar. "Joe," she called.

Stacey watched Joe bend over to pick up Piper. Her heart melted. Joe was going to love Piper. Her baby was finally going to have a daddy. It seemed to take hours, but Stacey finally reached her groom and touched his shoulder.

He turned, but her groom wasn't Joe.

It was Colton.

Alarm rushed through her.

Stacey awakened in a sweat. *Joe? Colton?* This couldn't be. "Colton," she whispered aloud and sat up in her bed. Why was she dreaming of Colton? Why was she even thinking of him? He was her neighbor, her best friend's brother. Ridiculous, she told herself. Beyond ridiculous. She shook her head and tried to push away the image of the tall, sexy cowboy.

Stacey forced herself to relax. She'd learned to seek sleep when her baby slept. Taking several deep breaths, she told herself not to think about Colton. She shouldn't think about his wide shoulders and his insanely curly, dark eyelashes. She shouldn't think about his strong jaw and great muscles and dependability. He was the kind of man who would always stand beside a friend and support him or her.

Colton was also a man who was clearly interested in another woman at the moment. Why else would he have sought Rachel's help about what women really want?

The reality of that made Stacey feel a little cranky, although, for the life of her, she couldn't say why.

"Go to sleep," she told herself. She would be so busy tomorrow with Piper that she would truly regret one minute of sleep she'd lose thinking about Colton.

The next day, just after Stacey put Piper down for her afternoon nap, she heard a knock at the front door. She knew that her mother had gone to a sewing circle meeting and her father was outside working, so she wanted to catch whoever was at the door before they awakened Piper. Heaven knew, Stacey cherished nap time.

She raced toward the front door and whisked it open. Colton stood on the front porch holding a pie. Surprise and pleasure rushed through her. "Well, hello to you. Come on inside."

"I can't stay long. My mother fixed a batch of

apple pies, and she thought your family might enjoy one," he said, following her.

"We certainly will. This will go great with the dinner I'm fixing tonight. Please, tell her I said thank you. Would you like some coffee?" she asked.

"No need," he said. "I really can't stay long. You're fixing dinner, you say? Do I smell pot roast?"

"You do," she said, and took the pie to the kitchen and quickly returned. "Since I'm not bringing home the bacon right now, I try to help around the house as much as possible. I fix dinner and clean while Piper naps. It's the least I can do. I'm also thinking about doing some after-school tutoring in math and science. I can have kids come here and Piper's not walking yet. I hear once the babies start walking, it's a whole different ballgame."

"I'm sure it is," he said.

Stacey looked up at Colton and noticed his eye-lashes again. When had he become sexy-looking? she wondered. Although she'd certainly always known Colton was male, she just hadn't thought of him as a man. And she shouldn't be thinking that way now either.

The silence stretched between them, and Stacey felt heat rush to her face. "Are you sure I can't get you a cup of coffee? It's the least I can do with you bringing over a pie."

"Trust me. I didn't bake that pie," he said in a dry tone. "But I'll take a cup if you're insisting. I'll be working outside, and it won't hurt to get warmed up before I face the cold."

"Just a moment," she said, and returned to the kitchen to pour Colton's coffee. As she reentered the den, she gave him the cup. "Any problems or just the regular endless chores?"

He nodded. "I need to do a little work on some fences. My dad's back isn't what it used to be, so I try to tackle anything that may cause him pain."

"That's nice of you," she said. "He refuses to go to the doctor, doesn't he?"

Colton nodded again. "He doesn't believe in it. Says it's a waste of time and money. The last time he went to the doctor, he nearly died from a burst appendix. And we almost had to beat him into going."

"I remember when that happened," Stacey said. "It was a long time ago. I'm sure someone has told him that there have been huge advances made in medical science."

"All of us have told him that, but he'd rather eat nails than admit he's hurting."

"Maybe you can persuade him to go to the doctor if you take him out for lunch in Vicker's Corners sometime," she suggested.

"Possible," he said. "Rachel might have better luck with him than I would. He has always let her get away with murder."

Stacey laughed. "She would disagree and give you half a dozen examples of when she has gotten in trouble. But even I know he has been harder on you."

"Yeah," he said. "But I always felt as if I had good parents. I'm sure you feel the same way, too."

"True," she said. "My father can be a little remote sometimes, but he's as solid as they come. After I had Piper, both my parents insisted I come back here to live with them." A slice of guilt cut through her. "I just wish I could give Piper what I had growing up." She felt the surprising threat of moisture in her eyes and blinked furiously. "It just wasn't meant to be."

Colton squeezed her arm. "Don't be so hard on yourself. From where I sit, it looks as if you're doing a dang good job. That baby is surrounded by people who love her. That's more than a lot of kids can say."

The tight feeling in her chest eased just a little from his words of encouragement. "Thanks. I have my share of doubts."

"Well, stop your doubting. You've got a healthy baby, and she's doing great," he said. "Besides that, you've got a slice of Olive Foster's famous apple pie in your future tonight."

"The only way I'll get a slice is if I hide it until after the meal," she said.

"Well, that's a no-brainer," he said, and leaned toward her in a way that seemed much sexier than it should. "Hide the pie. Indulge yourself."

Stacey's heart raced at Colton's instruction. A naughty image of how she could indulge herself with Colton raced through her mind, but she immediately slammed the door on her thoughts. After all, the last time she'd indulged herself she'd gotten pregnant.

Chapter Three

"I'm sorry I can't go with you," Rachel said to Stacey on her cell phone. "My friend Abby called me at the last minute to babysit, and it's her anniversary."

"I understand. You and I can catch up later," Stacey said, even though she dreaded attending Ella Mae Jergen's baby shower. Ella Mae was married to a hotshot surgeon, and the couple owned houses in both Lubbock and in the next town past Horseback Hollow. Ella Mae was pregnant with her first baby. The shower was a big deal for Horseback Hollow because Ella Mae had been born and raised there and her parents still lived in town. The shower was being held in the Jergen's mansion in the next town. Stacey couldn't help feeling intimidated.

Ella Mae, however, had been supportive of Stacey and had attended the shower for Piper, so Stacey was determined to return the favor.

"What's wrong?" her mother asked as Stacey put a pot of beans on for dinner while she held Piper on her hip.

"Nothing," Stacey said.

"Doesn't sound like nothing to me," Jeanne said, and put a lid on the beans. "Let me hold my grandbaby."

All Stacey had to do was lean toward her mother, and Piper extended her chubby little arms to her Gabby. Stacey checked the chicken and vegetables. "Looking good," she murmured.

"You don't have to cook every night," her mother said as she clucked over Piper.

"I'm not contributing to the household with green stuff, so I want to contribute in other ways," Stacey said.

"I don't want you overdoing it," her mother said.

"I'm not. I'm young and healthy," she said.

"That sounds like something I said when I was younger," her mother said. "You still didn't answer my question about your conversation with Rachel."

Stacey sighed. "Ella Mae's baby shower is tonight."

A brief silence followed.

"Oh," her mother said, because she knew that the Jergens were wealthy and anything they did had to be, oh, so perfect. "Do you want me to go with you?"

Her mother's offer was so sweet that it brought

tears to her eyes. Stacey put down her spoon and went to her mother to hug her. "You're the best mother in the world. You know that, don't you?"

Jeanne gave Stacey a big squeeze, then pulled back with a soft chuckle. "What makes you say that?"

"Because you always do the right thing. I wonder if I can do half as many right things as you have," Stacey said, looking into her mother's eyes and wishing that just by looking, she could receive all of her mother's wisdom.

Her mother slid her hand around Stacey's shoulders and gave her another squeeze. "You're already doing the right thing. Look at this gorgeous, healthy baby. You're a wonderful mother."

"Thanks, Mom," Stacey said, feeling as if she'd just received the highest praise possible.

"You don't have to go to Ella Mae's baby shower. Just drop off a gift," her mother said.

"No," Stacey said with a firm shake of her head. "She came to my shower. I should go to hers."

Jeanne pressed her lips together. "If you're sure…"

"I am," Stacey said. "And you already said you don't mind watching Piper. Right?"

"Not at all," her mother said. "You don't ask me often enough. I love my little Piper girl."

Stacey's heart swelled with emotion. "I'm so blessed," she said.

"Yes, you are," her mother said. "Now go get ready for Ella Mae's shower. You hold your head high. Don't forget it. You've done the right thing, and you're a good mother. Just make sure you're the second one out the door."

Stacey looked at her mother in confusion. "Second one out the door?"

"I never told you this before, but if you ever go to a party that you don't want to attend, then you can be the second one to leave. You don't want to be the first, but being the second is fine," her mother said.

Another word of wisdom Stacey swore to remember. "I'll be watching for who leaves first."

"And if anyone starts making insinuating comments about Joe, then pull out Piper's baby pictures. That should shut them up right away."

Stacey smiled at her mother. "Thanks, Mom."

Stacey raced to her room to pull on a black dress and boots. She put on some lip gloss and concealer, then threw on a colorful scarf and her peacoat.

"See you later, Mom," she called, then headed for her Toyota. Thank goodness snow and sleet had stayed away from Horseback Hollow during the past week. She started her car and got to the end of the driveway before she realized she had forgotten the gift for Ella Mae's baby.

Stacey backtracked and collected the gift, then returned to her trusty car. She headed out of Horseback Hollow toward the next town, then took several turns down several back roads until she reached the gated driveway for Ella Mae's house. The gate lifted to allow her entrance, and Stacey rode down the paved drive to the front of the Jergen mansion.

The windows of the house were lit, and the front door was open. Stacey knew what she would find inside. A crystal chandelier and exquisite high-profile designer furniture and decor.

Stacey was accustomed to homemade decorations and freshly painted rooms. Mama Jeanne decorated her home with family photos and mementos. The Joneses' home was warm and welcoming, but furniture had been chosen for durability, not how pretty it was.

A man approached Stacey as she paused in the driveway. "May I park your car, ma'am?"

Stacey blinked. "Excuse me?"

"Yes, ma'am. I'm the valet for the evening," he said.

Stacey blinked again. Heaven help her. *Valet? Don't fight it,* she told herself. *Let him park the car.* She would have to park her own all the nights thereafter, and that was okay.

Stacey accepted a nonalcoholic basil-something cocktail. She would have preferred a beer. She joined in with the socializing and the games and predicted that Ella Mae would have a boy. Stacey suspected that Ella Mae's husband would want a boy right off the bat, so she hoped Ella would be able to seal the deal with a male child.

When it came time for the big reveal of the baby's sex, it was done via cake. Blue. Stacey had been correct. Everyone cheered.

Ella Mae circled the room with her posse and stopped to visit with Stacey.

"I'm so glad you could come," Ella Mae said. "I know you've been busy with your baby."

"So true," Stacey said. "You'll learn soon enough."

"Well, I'll have help," Ella Mae said. "I'll have a husband and a nanny."

Stacey lost her breath. She felt as if she'd been slapped. She took a careful breath and remembered what her mother had said. She pulled out her cell phone. "Have you seen my Piper? She's just gorgeous, don't you think?" she asked as she flipped through the photos.

"What a darling," one of Ella Mae's friends said. "She's beautiful."

Stacey nodded. "And good as gold."

A couple moments later Ella Mae and her pack moved on. Stacey watched the door and saw two guests leave. It was time for her to go. On the drive home she decided to stop at the Superette to pick up some bananas for Piper. Piper loved bananas. Luckily, the Superette had quite a few. Then she headed to the only bar in town, the Two Moon Saloon, with the intention of drinking half a beer. She would be fine driving after drinking a whole beer, but Stacey wouldn't risk anything. Since she'd become a mother, everything had changed. She couldn't take any chances.

She went to the bar and ordered a beer. The first time in nearly a year and a half. She took a sip and felt so guilty she asked for a glass of water. Sensing the gazes of several men on her, she sipped at her water and wondered if coming here had been a good idea after all.

The bartender put another beer in front of her. "The guy at the end of the bar bought this for you."

Stacey glanced down the bar but didn't recognize the man. "Oh, I can't accept it. I don't know him."

"I can't take it back," the bartender said.

Feeling extremely uncomfortable, Stacey took another sip of water and eyed the door.

"Fancy meeting you here," a familiar male voice said.

"Oh, thank goodness," she said, and stretched both of her hands toward Colton.

"Problem?" he asked, glancing down at her hands clutching his arm.

"I just went to Ella Mae Jergen's baby shower. She made a snarky comment about my missing baby daddy. I came here for a beer, but I couldn't make myself drink it. And some guy bought me another beer. Save me," she said.

Colton chuckled and gently extracted her fingers from his arm. "Hey, Phil, buy Stacey's admirer a beer on me."

"Thank you," she said. "I was just going to drink half a beer, but I felt guilty after the first sip. Do you know how long it's been since I had a drink at a bar?"

"Apparently too long," Colton said.

"Maybe," she said.

"You don't have to give up living just because you had a baby," he said.

She nodded, but she didn't really agree.

Colton lifted her chin with his finger. "Your life is not over. You can still have fun," he said.

"I have fun," she said, unable to resist the urge to squirm. "I have lots of fun with Piper."

Colton shot her a doubtful glance. "You need to start getting out more. And I don't mean baby showers."

Stacey lifted her eyebrows at Colton's suggestion. "You don't mean dating, do you?"

"You don't have to date. You just need to get out. You're acting—" He broke off.

Stacey frowned. "I'm acting how?"

Colton scrubbed his jaw. "I don't know how to say this."

"Well, spit it out," she said. "I want to know."

Colton sighed. "You're acting…old."

Stacey stared at him in disbelief. *"Old?"* she repeated. "I'm acting *old?*" She couldn't remember when she'd felt so insulted. "I'm only twenty-four. How can I be old?"

"I didn't say you *are* old," Colton said in a low voice. "I said you're *acting* old."

"Well, I have a baby now. I need to be responsible," she said.

"I agree, but you don't have to stop living your life," he said.

Stacey paused, thinking about what Colton had

told her. "You're Mr. Responsibility. I can't believe you're telling me to cut loose and be a wild woman."

"I didn't say you should be a wild woman. I just said you need to get out more," he said.

"Hmm," Stacey said. "I'm going to have to think about this." She paused. "I wonder who I could call if I decide to get out. If I decide I want to have half a beer."

"You can call me," Colton offered. "Remember, I'm Mr. Responsibility."

In her experience, Stacey knew that Colton *was* Mr. Responsibility. He always had been and she valued that quality in him now more than ever. But lately, when she looked at Colton, she couldn't seem to forget what it had felt like to dance in his arms on New Year's Eve. And that almost kiss they'd shared. Almost, but not quite. She wondered what a real kiss from him would feel like. Stacey almost wished he'd kiss her and she would be disappointed, so she could stop thinking about him so much.

The next day, Colton showed up unexpectedly at the Joneses' house. Stacey was happy to see him even though he seemed intent on asking her father's thoughts about some issue with the cattle. She brought Colton and her father some coffee. Colton tossed her a smile but kept talking with her father.

Stacey couldn't help feeling a little jealous of the time he was spending with her father. She knew Piper would awaken any moment, and her time would then be divided. *Hurry up, Dad.* But she knew the mental urging was useless. Her father was usually stone quiet, but when it came to talking about the ranch, once he got going, he didn't stop.

She checked her watch and felt her stomach clench as she waited for Piper to call out for her. Finally, her father took a potty break. *Hallelujah.*

"Better today?" Colton asked her as he headed for the door, where Stacey waited on the porch.

She nodded. "I guess so. Sorry if I freaked out on you last night."

"You didn't," he said. "It's like I said. You just need to get out more. I know your mama would be more than happy to watch Piper for you every now and then."

"I don't want to burden her," Stacey said as she stepped out of the front porch with him. "They've taken Piper and me in. I don't want to take advantage of them."

"You wouldn't ever do that," he said. "Listen, how about if I take you to the bar and grill in town? What's a good day for you?"

Surprise rippled through her. "Are you sure? I don't want to intrude on your, uh, relationship with your new girlfriend."

He hesitated a half beat. "She won't mind," he said. "When do you want to go?"

"I think Thursday may work. I'll have to ask Mama first. Can I get back to you?"

"Sure," he said, and squeezed her arm just like one of her brothers would. "Remember to smile."

She stared after him as he started to walk away. "Wait," she said, and he turned around. "Do I frown that much?"

He paused. "You used to seem a lot happier," Colton said. "I hate to see you so sad and burdened."

"My life is different now," she said.

"But is it sad?" he asked.

She took a deep breath and thought about his question. "Not really." She smiled. "I'll call you about dinner at the grill followed by a beer. I appreciate the pity date."

"It's no pity date," he said. "We've known each other a long time. We should be able to cheer each other up. You may have to do it for me sometime," he said.

"That's hard for me to imagine," she said.

"You never know," he said, and her father returned to the den, ready to talk ranching.

Stacey gazed at Colton. There was more to him than she'd ever thought. Stacey wondered what it would be like to go on a real date with Colton. She wondered how it would feel to be the object of his affection. Rolling her eyes at herself, she shook her head and went to the laundry room to wash another load of baby clothes.

The next day, Stacey played with Piper, after cleaning the house and fixing dinner. She couldn't help thinking about Colton's offer for an evening out.

It wouldn't be fancy, but it would be a relief. She debated calling him ten times over, then finally gave in. He didn't pick up, so she hung up. Five minutes later, she called again. He still didn't answer, but this time she left an answer.

A half hour later, he returned her call. "Hello?" she said as she stirred soup for dinner and held Piper on her hip.

"Need an escape?" Colton asked.

She gave a short laugh. "How did you know?"

"Saw the hang-up, then heard the desperation in your voice mail," he said.

"I'm not that desperate," she said, even though she really needed an evening out.

"I know. Everyone needs an escape hatch every now and then," he said.

"What's yours?" she asked.

"If I really want to get away, I can go into town or even Vicker's Corners," he said.

"But you don't have a baby," she said.

He chuckled. "That I don't," he said. "It won't be fancy. Tomorrow night okay? What time do you want me to pick you up?"

"Five-thirty," she said.

"Early night?"

She laughed. "These days I only do early nights," she said. "You have a problem with that?"

"None at all, I'll see you tomorrow at five-thirty." He chuckled. "Call me if you need to escape earlier."

Stacey couldn't help smiling. "I'll pace myself. Bye for now."

The following day, Stacey's afternoon fell apart. Piper woke up early from her nap, and Stacey feared she'd burned the baked spaghetti casserole. She was having a bad hair day, and Piper was so cranky, Stacey wasn't sure she should ask her mother to babysit for the evening.

"Are you teething, sweetie?" she asked Piper.

Piper's sweet face crumpled in pain. Stacey sighed. "Mama, she's so fussy. I'm not sure I should leave her with you."

Her mother extended her arms to Piper, but Piper turned away. "Oh, come on, you sugar," Jeanne said to Piper. "I'll take care of you. Rub your sore gums with something that will make you feel better."

"No rum," Stacey said.

"I wasn't thinking of rum," Mama Jeanne said with an innocent expression on her face.

"No whiskey," Stacey added.

"I would never numb a baby's gums with whiskey," her mother said. "But bourbon…"

Stacey sighed. "Let me find the Orajel. I should have given it to her earlier."

"You know what your doctors say. You need to stay on top of the pain. You've told me that too many times to count when my hip was hurting."

"You're right, Mama. I should have done better for Piper," she said, feeling guilty.

"Well, don't leap off a ledge. She's not suffering

that much," her mother said, snatching Piper from her arms. "Go put on some lipstick and blush. You look worn out."

Piper fussed and squabbled, but didn't quite cry. "You're sure you'll be okay?"

"I've had a lot more babies than you have, sweetheart," Jeanne said.

"I'm working hard to meet a high standard," Stacey muttered.

"Hold on there," her mother said, putting her hand on Stacey's arm. "You're a great mother. Don't let anyone tell you otherwise. I didn't have to take care of my babies by myself. I had your father to help me, and trust me, he walked the floor many times at night to comfort all of you."

"I just feel bad that Piper won't have the kind of mother and father I had," Stacey said.

"Piper's getting plenty of loving. Her mama needs to stop trying for sainthood. Enjoy your evening out. It will be good for you and your baby."

"If you say so," Stacey said.

"I do. Now, go put on some lipstick," she said.

"Colton won't care. He's just taking me out to be nice," Stacey said, halfway hoping her mother would deny it.

"Maybe so, but it will make you feel better. That's the important thing," her mother said.

"Right," Stacey said, and headed to her room to remake herself for a trip to the grill where she would eat a burger and fries. This was how her life had evolved. Her big exciting night within a month was a trip to the grill.

Pathetic, she thought, but couldn't deny she was just glad to get away from the ranch. She put on lipstick, a little blush and some mascara. At the last moment, she sprayed her wrists with perfume.

"Stacey," her mother called from down the hall. "Colton's here."

A rush of excitement raced through her, and she rushed down the hall. Colton stood there dressed in jeans, a coat and his Stetson. "Hi," he said. "You look nice."

"Colton is afraid of Piper," her mother announced.

"I'm not afraid of her," he corrected. "She just looks so happy in your arms that I don't want to disrupt her."

Stacey chuckled under her breath. "You can go after a bear on your ranch, but a baby brings you to your knees."

Colton scowled at her. "I can shoot a bear."

Both Stacey and her mother erupted with laughter. "We should give him a break," her mother said. "Y'all enjoy yourselves." She lowered her voice. "Drink a beer for me."

"Mama," Stacey said, shocked.

"Oh, stop. Even a mother of seven likes to kick up her heels every now and then. See you later," she said, and returned to the kitchen.

Stacey met Colton's gaze. "I never expected that."

"Me either," Colton said, then lifted his lips in a crafty grin. "But I liked it."

Colton helped her into his truck and drove into town. "So, have you figured out what you want on your burger? Cheese, onions, mustard…"

"Cheese, mustard, grilled onions and steak sauce," she said. "I don't need the whole burger. I want the bun and fixin's."

"And French fries?" he asked.

"Yes, indeed," she said.

"We can take the burger into the bar if you want your beer with your meal," he said.

"The bar is loud," she said. "I can have a soda or water with my burger. It will be nice to hear myself think."

"Does your baby scream that much?" he asked.

Stacey shook her head. "Piper's much better now that she's done with her colic. But now she's teething. I need to remember to soothe her gums. I forgot today."

"Must be hard. All that crying," he said.

"She sleeps well at night and usually takes a good long nap. I'm lucky she's not crawling right now. She's really a good baby, Colton. I could have it much harder," she said, wanting Colton to like Piper.

"Yeah," he said, but he didn't sound convinced.

"Is my Mama right? Are you afraid of Piper?" she asked in a singsong voice.

"I'm not afraid of a baby," he said, his tone cranky. "I just haven't been around babies very much."

Stacey backed off. She wanted the evening to be pleasant. "How do you like your burger?"

"As big as I can get it. Mustard, mayonnaise, onion, pickle, lettuce and tomato," he said.

"You can have half of mine," she offered.

"We'll see. Maybe your appetite will improve now that you're out of the pen," he said.

She laughed, but his teasing made her feel good. "You are so bad."

"And you are so glad," he said.

"Yeah," she said. She couldn't disagree.

Colton pulled into the parking lot of The Horseback Hollow Grill, and he helped her out of his truck. His gentlemanly manners made her feel younger and more desirable. They walked into the grill and had to wait a few minutes for a table. Maybe more than one person needed an escape tonight, Stacey thought.

They sat, ordered, and the server delivered their sodas. Stacey took a long, cool sip of her drink and closed her eyes. "Good," she said.

"Simple pleasures are the best," Colton said.

Stacey looked at Colton for a long moment and shrugged her shoulders. "So, talk to me about grown-up stuff."

His eyes rounded. "Grown-up stuff?" he echoed.

"Yes," she said. "Movies, politics, current events."

"Well, politicians are as crooked as ever. There are blizzards and tsunamis. Wait till summer and there will be hurricanes, mudslides and fires." He grimaced. "I hate to admit it, but I haven't seen a movie lately. Rachel is watching the reality shows. I watch a lot of the History Channel," he said.

"What about movies?" she asked. "Do you like James Bond?"

He nodded. "I did see the most recent one. Lots of action."

"And lots of violence," she said.

"Yeah, but the good guy wins."

"That's most important," she said, and the server delivered their meals.

"That was fast," she said.

"Burgers are what they are known for," Colton said, and took a big bite out of his.

Stacey took a bite of her own and closed her eyes to savor a burger someone else had cooked for her. "Perfect amount of mustard and steak sauce," she said. "But all I need is half."

"You sure about that?" Colton teased, taking another big bite.

"I'm sure," she said, and enjoyed several more bites of her burger. She ate a little more than half and stopped. "Oh, no. Now I'm full. How can I eat the fries? Let alone drink a beer?"

"You need to learn to pace yourself," Colton said as he stared at his fries.

Stacey liked the wicked glint in his eyes that belied his practical advice. "Maybe I should fix some fences. Maybe that would help my appetite," she said, unable to force herself to eat even one French fry.

"Relax. We can hit the bar in a few minutes. There's no rush. Rest your belly," he said.

Not the most romantic advice, but Stacey stretched and took a few deep breaths. "I may have to take lessons from you on pacing myself."

"I'm available for hamburger-eating pacing lessons," he said with a mischievous grin that made her stomach take an unexpected dip.

A few minutes later, Stacey gave up on her fries, and she and Colton walked to the connecting bar. Colton ordered a couple of beers, and Stacey took a sip. Country music was playing in the background. If she closed her eyes, she could almost time travel back to over a year ago when she and Joe had just gotten engaged. She'd been unbelievably happy. Her future had been so bright. She'd clearly been a big fool.

Stacey hiccupped. "Oh, my," she said and hiccupped again.

"Drink too fast?" he asked.

"I didn't think so," she said, but hiccupped again. "It's just been so long since I sat down and drank even half a beer."

"Maybe you need one of those sweet mixed drinks," he said. "I'm not sure the bartender here can do that for you."

"It depends on whether he has vodka or not. I'm pretty sure he doesn't keep cranberry juice on tap."

Colton laughed. "You're right about the cranberry juice. I see Greg Townsend over there. He's the president of the local ranchers' association. Do you mind if I have a word with him?"

"Please, go ahead," she said. "Let me catch my breath."

"I'll just be a minute," he said.

Stacey closed her eyes, took a breath and held it. She counted to ten. Memories of how foolish she'd been with Joe warred with her enjoyment of her evening with Colton.

"Can I buy you another beer?" an unfamiliar male voice asked.

Stacey opened her eyes to meet the gaze of a man she didn't know. "Excuse me?" she said. He was tall and wore a Stetson. He also had a beard. She wasn't a big fan of beards.

"Can I buy you another beer?" he repeated, extending his hand. "I'm Tom Garrison. I haven't seen you around here before. I work at the Jergen's ranch."

"Oh, I know the Jergens," she said and briefly shook his hand. "Well, I know Ella Mae."

"And you are?" he asked.

"Stacey," she said, suddenly noticing her hiccups had disappeared. "Stacey Jones. Stacey Fortune Jones," she added, because the Fortune part was still very new to her.

"A pleasure to meet you, Stacey Fortune Jones," he said. "I'm kinda new in town and a little lonely since it's winter. Maybe you could show me around."

"Oh," she said, shaking her head and feeling uncomfortable. "I'm super busy. I have a little baby."

She figured that would put him off. Most men were afraid of babies who weren't their own.

"I like babies," he said. "I'm good with them."

Stacey began to feel just a teensy bit nervous. She searched the room for Colton. "Good for you, but, like I said, I'm super busy."

"I don't see a ring on your finger. That must mean you're not taken," he said, moving closer.

"Well," she said, trying to shrink against her bar stool. She wished Colton would return. He would know how to take care of this pushy man. "Like I said, I'm extremely busy..."

"I could give you a good time," he said. "Make you laugh. Maybe more..."

"Or not," Colton said, suddenly appearing next to the pushy cowboy. "She's with me."

Stacey breathed a sigh of relief.

"She was sitting here all by herself when I saw her," Tom said.

"For all of two and a half minutes. Go stalk someone else," Colton said. "Trust me, she's not your type."

"She's everybody's type," Tom grumbled, but walked away.

"Hmm," Colton said. "Can't leave you alone for even two minutes. There you go, seducing the new locals."

"I didn't seduce anyone," she protested. "I was just trying to get rid of my hiccups." She frowned. "I think my beer is flat."

"You want another one?"

"No. I just want to go home," she said and stood. "I'm glad you came back when you did. This was good enough for me. I won't be wondering how the other half lives. I'd rather eat a meal I've prepared and watch a good TV show." She met his gaze with a lopsided smile. "I'm getting old, aren't I? An old mama."

Colton shook his head. "Nah. You're just growing up. And you're the hot kind of mama, so keep up your guard."

Chapter Four

Colton wasn't sure his evening out with Stacey had been all that successful. She'd been quiet on the way home. He was bummed that he hadn't been able to cheer her up more. He wondered if he'd made things worse. He focused on his work at the ranch during the next couple of days and avoided the inquiring glances from the rest of his family.

As he drove home after a long day outdoors, his cell phone rang. It was Stacey. He immediately picked up. "Hey. What's up?"

"I'm trying to find Rachel," Stacey said. "I need her help."

"I'm just pulling into the drive. Let me see if I can find her and I'll call you back," he said.

Colton strode into the house and called for his sister. "Rachel," he called. "Rachel."

No answer. His parents didn't even respond.

He looked through the house and called a few more times. Sighing, he stabbed out Stacey's cell number. "Hey," he said. "No sign of Rachel or my parents."

"Darn," Stacey said. "My parents have gone to a town meeting."

"Oh, mine must have gone to the same meeting. This place is like a ghost house," he said and chuckled. "I think my voice may be echoing off the walls."

"Oh, bummer," Stacey said.

He heard the despair in her voice. "What's wrong?"

"Rachel was my last hope since my parents are out, and my sister Delaney isn't feeling well."

"Last hope for what?" he asked, pacing the hallway in his house.

"Well, you know my brother Toby took in three foster kids," she said. "He called me tonight and said the youngest is feeling bad. He has no experience with sick kids, so he asked me to come over and I said I would. But I don't want to expose Piper to anything. I don't want her to get sick."

"Yeah," Colton said. "That's rough."

She sighed. "I hate to leave Toby hanging. Would you mind watching her for a little while so I could help him out?"

Colton froze. The idea of taking care of a baby

terrified him. He could do a lot of things, but he had no experience with babies. But he couldn't leave Stacey in such a bind, could he? Well, darn. He inhaled. "Okay, I'll do it, but you need to give me lots of instructions. This isn't like roping a calf."

"She'll be easy. I promise. I'll write down lots of instructions and put them in the diaper bag," Stacey said. "I can't tell you how much I appreciate this."

"Yeah," Colton said, and headed back to his car. It occurred to him that he would rather get stomped by a bull than take care of a baby.

He drove his truck the short distance to the Joneses' ranch and pulled in front of the house. His family had celebrated with the Jones family many times. Their home was as familiar to him as his own.

But a baby wasn't familiar to him at all.

Colton ground his teeth, then forced himself to present a better attitude. He could handle this. He'd handled far more difficult situations. Piper was just a six-month-old baby. How hard could it be, he asked himself, but he was sweating despite the freezing temperature outside.

He stomped up the porch steps and lifted his hand to knock on the door, but it swung open before his knuckles hit wood. Stacey looked up at him with a hopeful expression on her face as she held her baby on her hip. "She should go to sleep soon," Stacey said. "She's just a little worked up tonight."

"Worked up," he repeated, feeling more uneasy.

Stacey fluttered her hands. "Oh, it won't last

long," she said. "She'll get tired. Let me grab my coat, and I'll be back before you know it."

She thrust Piper into his hands. He stared at the baby, and she stared back at him. Mistrust brewed from his side, and he saw the same mistrust in the baby's eyes. "What am I supposed to do with her?" he asked.

"Rock her, walk her. Feed her only if you're desperate because she's already been fed." Stacey buttoned a peacoat and handed him a diaper bag. "This is my complete bag of tricks," she said. "This will be a breeze. You're going to surprise yourself. Trust me. Thank you so much," she said, and rushed out the door.

Colton resisted the urge to renege. Barely. After Stacey was gone, he looked at Piper. She let out a little wail. Colton dived into the diaper bag, skipped everything and went straight for the bottle.

Piper sucked it down, then stared at him and gave a loud, powerful burp.

"Whoa," Colton said, backing away from the sound. "How'd you do that?"

Piper squirmed and fussed.

Colton bobbed up and down. "Hey. Your tummy's full. You should be better."

Piper whined in response.

Colton grimaced. He had been hoping food would be the quick fix. It usually was for him. He patted her back and continued to walk. Piper whined and occasionally wailed. Colton had no idea how to please the baby.

Oh, wait. Maybe she had a messy diaper.

Eewww, he thought. He didn't want to change a diaper. That was just too gross. But maybe that would turn the trick and the baby would stop fussing.

Groaning to himself, Colton went to the magic diaper bag and pulled out a diaper, a packet of wipes and a changing pad. "Okay. Okay," he said to Piper as he set her down on the pad. "Give me a break. This is my first time."

Piper stuck her fingers in her mouth and gazed up at him with inquisitive green eyes.

At least she wasn't crying, he thought and lifted her gown. "Okey, doke. We can do this," he said because some part of him remembered that he'd seen a few people talk to babies. It wasn't as if they understood. Maybe they just liked the sound of a human voice.

Who knew?

He looked at the diaper, and for the life of him, he couldn't figure out which was the front and the back.

Piper began to squirm and make noises. They weren't fussy, but they were getting close.

"I'm getting there," he promised. "Just give me a little extra time."

He pulled open the dry diaper, then carefully unfastened the baby's dirty diaper. Colton glimpsed a hideous combination of green, yellow and brown.

"Oh, Piper. How could you?"

The baby squirmed and almost seemed to smile. Heaven help him.

Colton pulled out a half dozen wipes and began rubbing her front and backside. Six wipes weren't enough, so he pulled out some more and cleaned her a little more. Afterward, he tossed some baby powder on her and put on the disposable diaper.

Sweat was dripping from his forehead. "There. We did it."

Piper began to fuss.

"Well, thanks for nothing," he said, picking up her and the dirty diaper. He wondered if there was a special hazardous-waste disposal container in the house for the baby's diapers. He didn't see one, so he tossed it in the kitchen trash and felt sorry for the poor fool who lifted the lid to take out the garbage.

He jiggled Piper, but she was still fussy. He wondered if he shouldn't have fed her. He cruised the hallways of the house. Piper never broke into a full cry, but he could tell she was right on the edge.

Desperate, he tried to sing. "Mamas, don't let your babies—"

Piper wailed.

"Not a good choice," he muttered and jiggled her even more. He walked and talked, since talking worked better than singing did. She calmed slightly, but he could tell she still wasn't happy. This female was definitely difficult to please.

After thirty minutes, she was still fussy and Colton was growing desperate. He headed for the magic diaper bag and sat down to dig through it. Piper sobbed loudly in his ear as he searched the bag.

"Give me a break," he said. "I'm trying." He dug his way all the way to the bottom and grabbed hold of a bottle. Pulling it out, he stared at a bottle labeled, "Last resort".

Colton was pretty sure he was at his last resort. He opened the bottle and found a wand. "Well, damn," he said, and began to blow bubbles.

Piper immediately quieted and stared at the bubbles.

Colton continued to blow, and Piper began to laugh. It was the most magical sound he'd ever heard. He blew the bubbles, and she giggled. Her reaction was addictive.

"Well, who would have known?" he muttered under his breath. Maybe everyone should come armed with a bottle of bubbles. He blew bubbles past the time he was tired from it, and Piper finally rested her head on his shoulder. Colton wasn't taking any chances, though, and he kept up his bubble blowing.

Finally, he glanced down and saw that Piper's eyes were closed—half moons with dark eyelashes fanned against her creamy skin. She was one beautiful kid, he thought. The spitting image of Stacey. He gently strolled through the hallways again.

Weariness rolled through him. He'd been up before dawn and trying to work through a mile-long list of chores his father shouldn't do. The sofa in the den beckoned him. He wondered if he could possibly sit down without waking Piper.

Colton decided to give it a shot. He slowly eased down onto the sofa. Piper squirmed, and he froze. *Don't wake up,* he prayed. He waited, then leaned back, inch by inch. "We're okay," he whispered. "We're both okay."

Colton relaxed against the side of the sofa and slinked down. He rested his head backward and moved the baby onto his chest. "Don't wake up." He rubbed her back until he fell asleep.

"Stick out your tongue, Kylie," Stacey said to her brother's youngest foster child.

Redheaded Kylie reluctantly stuck out her tongue. Stacey saw no signs of strep. "I'm sorry you feel bad, sweetie," she said.

"I can stick out my tongue," Kylie's older brother, Justin, said and fully extended his tongue from his mouth. The boy's expression had a disturbing resemblance to a rock singer.

"Not necessary, but thanks, sweetie," she said.

Stacey turned to her brother Toby. "Her temperature is normal, and her lymph nodes feel fine. I would give her some extra liquids and try to help her get some extra rest." She rubbed Kylie's arm. "Do you feel achy?" she asked.

Kylie shook her head. "No, but my head hurts."

"I'm so sorry," Stacey said. "I bet a cool washcloth would feel good. If she can't sleep, she can take some children's Tylenol. In the meantime, Kylie needs some rest, comfort and cuddling."

"Does that mean I get to use the remote for the TV?" Kylie asked.

Stacey laughed. "I think you are definitely due the remote."

"But I wanna see SpongeBob," Justin said.

"You can see SpongeBob anytime," Toby said, rubbing Justin's head. "Let's just pile on the couch and watch what Kylie wants to watch."

Her brothers sighed but scrambled onto the couch. "I hope it's not a princess movie," Brian, the eleven-year-old, said.

"I want *Monsters,*" Kylie said.

"Again?" Brian said in disgust.

"Kylie gets to choose tonight. If you don't like her choice, you can get ahead on your homework or read a book," Toby said.

Stacey did a double take. She still couldn't quite get used to seeing her bachelor brother turn into an instant dad by agreeing to take on these three kids. Then again, Toby had always had a generous heart, so she really shouldn't be surprised. Stacey knew he'd met the kids when he'd volunteered at the Y. When he'd learned their mother had died at an early age and that their father wasn't around, he'd tried to give them some extra encouragement. When their situation had gone from bad to worse and the aunt who'd been caring for them was forced into rehab,

Toby had stepped forward to take them into his house by becoming a foster dad.

"Well, I'd better head back to the house. I couldn't find anyone except Colton to take care of the baby while I was gone," she said, packing up her little medical bag.

"Colton?" Toby echoed, giving a startled laugh. "You asked Colton Foster to take care of Piper?"

Stacey lifted her hands. "He was my only choice. Everyone else was busy, and I didn't want to leave you in the lurch."

Toby sighed. "Well, tell him I said thank you. I'll feel better about Kylie now that you've checked her."

"You still need to keep an eye on her. You should check her temperature and symptoms in the morning. It's a shame the kids' regular doctor is out of town," she said. "I wish we had a clinic in Horseback Hollow. Maybe I could get a job there," she said. "That's wishful thinking," she murmured, then looked up at her brother and squeezed his arm. "Are you okay?"

"Yeah," Toby said, but raked his hand through his hair. "This situation definitely has its ups and down. It all goes along smoothly for a few days, then it seems like we hit a big bump in the road."

Stacey pulled on her coat and walked to the door. "Regrets?" she asked in a low voice.

Toby shook his head firmly. "I did the right thing, and they're good kids. They make me laugh every day."

"Well, I admire you, Toby. Not many men would

do what you've done," she said. Three kids, all red-heads with tons of energy.

"I think I'm getting a lot more out of this than I expected," he said.

She gave her brother a big hug. "Call me anytime, and bring the kids over to visit Piper. When they're well," she quickly added.

"I'll do that," he said and opened the door. "Drive safely," he instructed, protective as ever.

"Good night. Get that cool washcloth for Kylie. See if it helps," she called over her shoulder and got into her car.

Stacey drove toward her house, growing more nervous with each increasing mile she covered. It wasn't that Piper was a bad baby, but at times she could be demanding and very vocal. Stacey hoped the baby had calmed down enough to fall asleep. She supposed that if Colton had really needed anything, he would have called her. As she pulled in front of the house, the lights from inside welcomed her. She got out of the car, climbed the stairs and opened the door.

She paused for a long moment, listening for the sound of Piper. All she heard was quiet. Stacey breathed a sigh of relief. Piper must have fallen asleep. She was surprised the television wasn't on. She would have expected Colton to turn on a ball-game once he'd put Piper in her crib.

Stepping into the den, she caught sight of Colton napping on the sofa with Piper asleep on his chest. Her heart swelled with emotion. If that wasn't the sweetest sight she'd ever seen, she thought. Seeing her daughter being held by a good strong man reminded Stacey of everything Piper was missing on an everyday basis. Tears filled her eyes, and she blinked furiously to keep them at bay.

First things first, she thought. Get the baby to bed. She gingerly extracted Piper from Colton's chest, praying the baby wouldn't awaken. Then she tiptoed to the small nursery in the room next to hers and put Piper down in her crib. Piper gave a few wiggly moves, and Stacey held her breath. Then the baby sighed and went back to sleep.

Stacey returned to the den and touched Colton's shoulder. He didn't awaken. She gave him a gentle shake, then another. The man was dead to the world. He must be worn out, she thought. He'd probably put in a full day at the ranch, yet he'd still agreed to watch Piper for her.

A rush of sympathy flooded through her. Stacey had lived on a ranch long enough to know it involved hard backbreaking work and long hours. It wouldn't hurt him to rest a little longer, she thought, and pulled the blanket from the back of the sofa and put it over him.

Backing away, she pulled off her coat and hung it in the closet, then returned to the den. Sinking onto the chair across from the sofa, Stacey allowed herself the luxury of looking at Colton while he was unaware. She wondered why she'd never noticed how attractive he was before. Sure, she'd known him her entire life, but she wasn't blind.

He was as strong as they came. Broad shoulders and she'd bet he might even have a six-pack. She blushed at the direction her mind was headed. He had a bit of stubble on his chin. His hard masculinity was at such odds with those eyelashes, she thought.

She wondered what it would be like to sleep with him and wake up with him. Would he be grouchy or sweet in the morning? She wondered what kind of lover he would be. She'd only had one, Joe. Their lovemaking sessions had often felt rushed to her, and although it wasn't something she discussed, she'd never felt completely, well, satisfied after sex with Joe.

Stacey wondered if Colton was the kind of man to take his time with a woman. Although she hadn't paid much attention, she'd heard of more than one woman he'd left more than happy after a night together. Lately, she was becoming much more curious about Colton. She kept reminding herself that he was interested in someone else, but that didn't seem to take the edge off her...curiosity.

At that moment, she heard the front door open and her father talking to her mother. "That meeting went on forever," he grumbled.

"Everyone has a right to speak their mind," Jeanne said.

"Well, they could speak a little faster," he said, and closed the door firmly behind him.

Stacey saw Colton jolt awake at the sound. He glanced around. "What the—" He broke off and shook his head.

"Hi," she said.

"Hey," he said, rising quickly.

"Listen, thank you for taking care of Piper," she said, also getting to her feet.

"No problem," he said, rubbing his face. "I guess I'll head home—"

Her mother and father entered the den. "Well, hello there, Colton. It's good to see you."

"Colton agreed to watch Piper while I checked out Kylie for Toby. He said she wasn't feeling well and their doctor is out of town, so he wanted me to come over and make sure she was okay. She just had a headache. I think Toby may be a little nervous fostering those three kids. Can't say I blame him."

"I'm glad Kylie is okay. It sure was nice of you to come over here and look after Piper," Jeanne said.

"That, it was. She can run you ragged at bedtime," her father said sympathetically.

"Daddy," Stacey said in an accusing tone.

"But she's a cute one and we love her," her father added.

"Of course we do," her mother said. "Why don't you join us for some hot chocolate before you leave? I can have it ready in no time."

"You don't need to do that," Colton said, appearing a bit embarrassed.

"I want to," Jeanne said. "Now sit down and relax,

and I'll have that hot chocolate for you before you know it."

Colton sighed and sat down on the edge of the sofa. "Is there anyone who can say no to your mother?"

"Not for long," Stacey said, laughing. "How was Piper?"

Colton nodded. "She did fine," he said in a non-committal tone.

Stacey read between the lines. "She was a beast, wasn't she? I was afraid of that. Even though I'd fed her, she seemed unsettled." Stacey sighed. "I'm sorry."

"I wouldn't call her a beast," Colton said. "Now," he added and chuckled, "amazing how something so small can get you so twisted trying to get her to calm down."

"How did you get her calm?" she asked, curious.

"You mean after I gave her the bottle in your magic bag and changed the toxic dump of her diaper?" he asked.

"Oh," she said, cringing.

"Yeah, I might need to take the kitchen trash out tonight before I leave," he said.

Her mother entered the room with cups of hot chocolate filled with mini-marshmallows. "This will help you sleep better once you get home, Colton," she said.

"I think Piper may have worn him out, so he may not need any help falling asleep," Stacey said.

"Oh, dear," her mother said, wincing. "She's gotten so much better during the last month. Did she have a rough night?"

"I wonder if she sensed that I was in a tizzy about getting over to Toby's house," Stacey said.

"Well, I speak from experience. Babies can sense our moods. Especially their mom's moods. At the same time, she may have just had a little tummy ache. Can I get you something to eat, Colton?"

"No, I'm fine, Mrs. Jones. Mrs. Fortune Jones," he corrected.

Her mother smiled. "That was sweet," she said. "But you've known me long enough to call me Jeanne." Her mother looked at Stacey. "Now, what on earth made you think to call Colton to take care of Piper?"

"I was trying to reach Rachel and she didn't pick up. I was hoping Colton could reach her," Stacey said.

"Oh," her mother said with a glance that combined intuition and suspicion. "Colton was definitely the man of the hour tonight, wasn't he?"

Uncomfortable with her mother's almost knowing expression, Stacey cleared her throat. "Yes, he was."

Chapter Five

A couple days later, Colton went into town to get some special feed and pick up a few things from the Superette for his mom. He would almost swear his mother could sense when he was headed into town because she always seemed to have a list of items for him to pick up from the small grocery—well, the only grocery—in town.

Using the term town might have been an exaggeration. Colton may have lived his entire life in Horseback Hollow, but he'd traveled enough to know his birthplace was more about wide open spaces than tall buildings and city conveniences. The *town* was just two streets long.

Colton glanced at the list his mother had given him and picked up apples, bananas, onions, tomato sauce and pasta. He hoped that meant spaghetti was in his near future. He added a can of green beans to his basket.

"Hey. What are you doing here?" a familiar voice spoke up from behind him. He turned and saw Stacey standing in the aisle.

"Just picking up a few things," he said. "What about you?"

"Formula and baby food for Piper," she said. "I just took something to the post office for Mom."

She glanced at his food items. "Spaghetti," she said more than asked. "Are you cooking for someone special?"

Confused, he cocked his head to one side. "Someone special?"

"Don't be shy," she said with a coy smile. "Cooking for your lady friend. I have a great recipe for spaghetti sauce, but you need sausage and cheese," she said.

He shrugged. "I haven't ever fixed spaghetti before unless it was from a can."

"Well, you've got to do better than that for a woman. If you're cooking for two, you could add some delicious bread and salad and call it good," she said. "And something chocolate. Women love chocolate."

Colton opened his mouth to protest, but she didn't let him fit a word in edgewise.

"I could help you," she offered. "Why don't I give you a cooking lesson? If you're anything like my brothers, you've relied on your mother your entire life for your meals, so you never bothered to learn."

That was a little insulting, he thought. But true.

"You sure you won't tell me who you're cooking for?" she asked.

"My lips are sealed," he said. It was easy to keep that secret since his so-called lady love didn't exist.

She gave a little huffy sigh. "Okay, well, I can still give you a few tips on your cooking. Is tonight okay?"

"I guess," he said, trying to recall his parents' busy schedule. He thought they were playing bridge tonight.

"Okay, I'll see you around six, and I'll help you fix a spaghetti dinner that will wrap your lady friend around your little finger. Make sure you pick up some sausage and fresh Parmesan cheese. I'm assuming you already have beef," she said.

"Yeah," he said. He lived on a cattle ranch. He darned well should have beef.

"Okay. See you later," she said and strode away.

Colton stared after her, distracted by the wiggle in her walk and her cute backside. He gave himself a shake. Why had he agreed to a cooking lesson? Especially for the sake of his imaginary girlfriend? He swore under his breath. This was getting worse and worse.

Stacey paid at checkout and walked to her car with her purchases. She felt a little cranky and wasn't sure why. Climbing into her car, she started the engine and headed for her house. She turned on the radio to listen to a few tunes to cheer herself up. It didn't quite work, though. Seeing Colton at the Superette purchasing food to feed the woman he clearly had a crush on made her grind her teeth. It must be nice to have a man work that hard to please you, she thought. She wouldn't know because no man had ever tried that hard to make her happy.

Frowning, she tried to push aside her feelings. It wasn't as if she wanted Colton to be cooking for her. Even though she'd looked at him with a little lust the other night, she'd decided that was an aberration. She couldn't really believe that she wanted Colton. Stacey told herself she was just lonely for some attention. That had to be it.

She returned home and unloaded her car while Piper napped.

"Are you sure you're okay?" her mother asked. "You're awfully quiet."

"I'm fine. Do you mind watching Piper for a little while tonight?"

"Of course not. Do you have plans?"

"I, uh, offered to give Colton a cooking lesson. He said he's trying to cheer up an unnamed female," she confessed.

Her mother lifted her eyebrows. "Oh, my," she said. "How generous of you. You know Colton keeps such a low profile. It's easy to underestimate him as, well, a romantic possibility."

"Not really," Stacey said. "I've heard some rumors about girls that liked him just fine."

"Oh, really," her mother said and paused. "Well, I think you're very sweet to help him prepare a dinner for another woman."

"I'm not doing that," Stacey snapped, then deliberately took a breath. "I'm just giving him a cooking lesson. He's like all my brothers except Toby. He can't cook worth a darn because his mother has cooked for him his entire life."

Her mother tilted her head. "Are you criticizing me for cooking for my family?"

Stacey closed her eyes and smiled, shaking her head. She went to her mother and gave her a big hug. "Of course not. You're the best mother any of us could have. But you have to admit those boys like having their meals put in front of them."

"You're right about that," she said ruefully and returned Stacey's embrace.

Stacey's cell phone rang, and she pulled it out of her purse. She didn't recognize the number. "Stacey Fortune Jones," she answered.

"Stacey, this is Sawyer. We have a situation here at the flight school. We need your help."

Stacey's pulse picked up. "What's wrong?"

"There's been an accident. My pilot Orlando has been hurt. The paramedics are on the way, but it will take a while, and the doctor's not in town."

"Oh, that's right," she said, remembering the same doctor who took care of Toby's foster children covered the whole town. "I'll be right there," she said, and turned to her mother. "I have to go. There's been an emergency at the flight school."

"Oh, no," her mother said. "Is it serious?"

"I think so," Stacey said grimly as she ran to her room to grab her medical bag.

Pulling into the flight school, she stopped her car and ran toward the figures beside the burning plane. Stacey went into nurse mode when she assessed Orlando Mendoza. She checked his blood pressure and pulse and noted that the pilot kept going in and out of consciousness. He'd likely suffered a concussion, and she could see he'd sustained a compound fracture of his left leg and another fracture of his left arm, so she made a temporary brace for each to prevent unnecessary movement and loss of blood. Although she was able to stabilize him until the paramedics arrived, she couldn't be certain that he hadn't suffered internal injuries, as well.

Stacey watched the ambulance drive away from the airport, then returned home and took a quick shower. The entire time, she kept thinking about Orlando Mendoza. She'd wished she could do more for him, but it was a miracle he'd survived the crash. She checked in on Piper and her mother and answered Mama Jeanne's twenty questions about the accident. Unfortunately, Stacey wasn't sure how everything would turn out for Orlando. This was one more reason Stacey wished there was an emergency facility closer to Horseback Hollow. Her hair still wet, she put it on top of her head and headed out the door to go to the Fosters' house.

After driving the few minutes to the Fosters, Stacey raced to the porch and knocked on the front door. "I'm sorry I'm late," she said when Colton answered the door. "Did you hear about the accident at the flight school?"

He shook his head. "I just got in from the field. What happened?"

"One of the planes from the flight school went down and the pilot was injured. Orlando Mendoza. The paramedics were taking a while to get there, so Sawyer asked me to come and do what I could to stabilize him."

"Oh, man," Colton said. "You think he'll make it?"

"I don't know. He was unconscious most of the time and he had a badly broken arm and leg," she said, her mind flashing back to a visual of the man.

"Hmm," Colton said. "Listen, you look pretty upset. We don't have to do this cooking lesson."

She shook her head. "I can't do anything now for him except pray. I could really use a distraction."

Colton gave a slow nod. "Okay," he said with a lopsided grin. "If teaching me how to fix Stacey's spaghetti will distract you, then that's what we'll do."

"Fine," she said and headed for the kitchen. "Let's start with chopping that onion. Some key things you need to know about making spaghetti are that you shouldn't overcook the noodles and you should break up the meat before you put it in the pan. But don't overwork it," she instructed.

"I'm taking mental notes," he said.

"You won't just be taking mental notes," she said. "You'll be doing the work. You remember what you do more than you remember what someone says."

"That sounds like something my father would say," he said.

"It's actually something my father once said," she said, and met his gaze. "It must be a conspiracy."

He chuckled. "You must be right."

"Wash your hands," she said.

"Yes, Mama," he said.

She shot him a disapproving look.

"Whoa," he said, lifting his hand in mock self-protection. "You've got lasers shooting from your eyes."

"One of my superpowers. Let's get to work," she said. She noticed that Colton possessed a much better sense of humor than Joe had. Not that she was comparing.

Stacey felt overly aware of Colton's physical presence in the kitchen as they prepared the meal. His shoulders grazed hers. Her hip slid against his. She put her hand over his to show him how to chop the onion. She couldn't help noticing his hands. They were large, but there was nothing awkward about the way he used them. For an instant, she couldn't help thinking about how his hands would feel on her body. The image heated her from the inside out.

Stacey tried to ignore her feelings. She helped Colton drain the pasta, and he was just way too close. Way too strong. And she was way too curious. She looked directly into his brown eyes and glimpsed a spark that mirrored hers.

She could have, should have looked away, but she didn't.

His nostrils flared slightly, and she couldn't tell if he was having the same problem with curiosity and self-restraint that she was. "This looks good," he said.

"It should be," she said, and turned away to stir the sauce. "It's best to cook this a longer time, but thirty minutes will do if you're in a rush." She lifted a spoonful of sauce and blew on it for a few seconds. She took a tiny taste. "Yum."

She offered him a sample from the same spoon. Colton covered her hand with his to steady the spoon and took a taste. He nodded. "That's good. Hard to believe I fixed it," he said with a half grin.

"Yes, it is," she said, and threw back her head in a laugh. "I'm surprised at how well you do in the kitchen."

"You never knew a lot of things about me," he said.

Her stomach took a dip to her knees, and her sense of humor suddenly vanished. "That's very true. Maybe you could say the same about what you know about me."

"Maybe I could," he admitted and stepped closer to her.

In theory, Stacey could have turned away. In reality, she probably should have. But she was just too curious and too, well, warm. She wanted to feel Colton Foster's chest against hers. She wanted to feel his arms around her. She wanted to feel his lips on hers.

Stacey gave in to all her bad urges and flung herself into Colton's arms. His hard chest against her breasts felt so much better than she'd expected. His arms around her gave her a melting sensation. And his kiss made her want so much more. How could his mouth be both firm and sensual? How could such a little taste of him send her into a frenzy?

She opened her mouth, and he took her with a kiss that sent her upside down. She couldn't resist the urge to wiggle against him. Colton gave a low groan that made her burn. She felt his hand travel to the small of her back to pull her even closer. She was breathtakingly aware of his hard body from his chest all the way down to his thighs.

Oh, yes, she thought. *More, give me more.*

The force of her need bowled her over. Panic raced through her. This was Colton, and she was getting ready to make a fool of herself.

Stacey pulled back, knowing her face was flaming red. She was embarrassed all the way down to her toes. "Oops. I should go. I really should go," she managed and refused to meet Colton's gaze. She wondered how she would survive this, but couldn't focus on that. She grabbed her coat and ran out the door.

Stacey drove home with her window down so she could cool off. Despite that, when she walked in the door she still felt as if she were on fire. Fanning her face, she pulled off her coat and threw it on a hanger.

She gnawed the inside of her lip as she walked toward the kitchen. She needed a very, very cold glass of water. She just wasn't sure if she was going to drink it or pour it over her head.

"Stacey?" her mother called from the den. "Is that you?"

She took a deep breath and tried to compose herself. She walked to the doorway of the den. "It's me. How was Piper?"

"No trouble at all," her mother said. Her father was sitting next to her, dozing on the sofa. "She fell asleep like that," her mother said, snapping her fingers and smiling.

"I'm glad to hear that. Thank you again for looking after her," Stacey said.

"You know I will look after her anytime," her mother said.

"Yes, but I don't want to take advantage of you," Stacey said.

"It's not taking advantage," her mother insisted. "It's my pleasure. Besides, I know you would never take advantage of me. Enough about that." She waved her hand. "So, how did the cooking lesson with Colton go?"

Stacey forced a smile. "Great. I think he's ready to fix my super spaghetti recipe all by himself."

"Good for him," her mother said. "You're a sweet girl to help him do that for another woman. Colton's a good man. I might not be as generous as you are."

Stacey managed to laugh. "I've known Colton forever. He's just like a brother."

"But he's not really a brother," her mother said, then shrugged. "Doesn't matter. Can I fix you some hot chocolate?"

"No, thanks, Mama. I think water will do. I'm off to bed," Stacey said, and went to the kitchen to get that tall glass of ice water. Maybe she should get two.

The next day, Stacey prepared enough food for a month of meals. Thank goodness, the Jones family had a big roomy freezer.

Her brother Jude dropped by before dinner. "Wow," he said, when he looked at all the casserole dishes on top of the counter. "Are we feeding the entire town of Horseback Hollow?" he asked.

Stacey shot him a quelling glance. "This would feed far more than the township of Horseback Hollow. Technically, we don't even live in the township of Horseback Hollow."

Jude shrugged his shoulders. "True, so why did you cook so much?"

Stacey considered keeping her feelings to herself,

but if anyone should understand, it would be Jude. Everyone knew he fell in love or like at the drop of a hat. She'd always thought of him as a Romeo. "I'm cooking to distract myself from something that's bothering me. I have a crush on Colton Foster," she whispered.

Silence followed. "Colton Foster? When did this happen?"

"Recently," she said. "I didn't plan it. And I think he has feelings for another woman."

"Who?" Jude asked.

She shook her head. "I don't know. He's been cagey about it."

"You've talked to him about another woman and you still have a crush on him?" he asked in disbelief.

"It didn't happen exactly like that. Don't fuss at me," she said. "I thought you would understand."

"Hell, no," Jude said. "Don't jump into a new romance. It's not in your best interest."

She gave a double take at his advice. "Says the guy who falls in love or like at least once a month."

"I don't want you to get hurt. Colton's a good guy, but if he's involved with another girl…"

"I didn't say he was involved," she said. "He just said he wanted to make her happy."

Jude winced. "That's a big deal, Stacey. Guys don't talk about making a woman happy if they aren't already pretty committed."

"Thanks for the encouragement," she murmured as she bundled up another casserole for the freezer.

Jude squeezed her shoulder. "I'm just looking out for you."

She took a deep breath. "I know. It just seems ironic for you to be warning me away from my feelings for Colton."

"Maybe I'm changing in my old age," he said. "Or maybe I just don't want you to get hurt again."

Stacey thought about Joe and frowned. "I know it may sound crazy, but I feel as if my engagement to Joe was a lifetime ago."

"I still wouldn't mind kicking him into next week," he said. "He shouldn't have abandoned you."

"He couldn't handle the commitment," she said, and only felt a twinge of sadness over the situation. She had begun to realize that Joe's abandonment was his issue more than hers. "It's taken a while for me to realize this, but I wouldn't want him if he stayed with Piper and me out of obligation. At the same time, I feel terrible that Piper doesn't have the daddy she deserves. But the truth is, I'm not sure Joe deserves her."

Jude studied her for a long moment. "Dang, girl. You've grown up."

She smiled at her brother. "You think?"

"Yeah," he said, and waggled his finger at her. "Just don't go falling for the local cowboys. I don't want you to get hurt." His gaze slid to the pot on the stove. "Can you share any of that soup? The smell is killing me."

"That bad, huh?" she asked, smiling at his description.

"Have a little pity," he said.

"Tell the truth," she said. "When was the last time you prepared a full meal for yourself or anyone else?"

"Grilled cheese and canned soup count?"

She shook her head.

He sighed. "A long time."

"That's what I thought," she said. "Maybe you're due for a cooking lesson."

"I'll tell you a secret, Stacey. It's my goal to never need to cook for myself. That is the goal of most bachelors," he said.

"Well, at least you're honest," she said, and planted a kiss on his cheek. She fixed a large container of soup for him to take home. She spent the next hour storing meals. Piper awakened, and Stacey gave her a half bottle of baby food and her bottle. Afterward, it was time for baby calisthenics. Stacey set Piper on her belly and watched her do dry swimming. Piper grunted and groaned as she exercised.

When Piper's groans turned to cries, Stacey whisked her up in her arms and walked to the kitchen with her. Stacey finished wrapping up her meals for storage and put a few portions in the refrigerator. Her father was always grateful when she packed a lunch he could take outdoors.

Tucking Piper into a baby pack, Stacey began to clean the public areas of the house. She took care of the den, foyer and kitchen and began to feel tired. Pulling Piper from the sack, Stacey sank onto a chair in the den and told herself not to think about Colton.

Even her Romeo brother, Jude, had warned her away from her feelings. But Stacey couldn't keep her mind off of Colton. She wanted to be close to him. Very close.

She concentrated on rocking Piper, then burping her. Stacey knew she needed to focus on Piper. Her baby needed her love and devotion.

Unfortunately, Stacey was all too aware of her own needs. How was she supposed to make those needs disappear?

The next afternoon while her mother made some calls to her circle group, Stacey folded laundry in the den. Piper took a nap. Stacey did the hated job of folding sheets. Was there any good way of folding fitted sheets? With the television on a news show, she folded several linens.

A knock sounded at the door, and she rushed to keep whoever was on her porch from knocking again. She didn't want Piper waking from the noise. It was amazing how precious her child's sleep had become to her, she thought. She wondered if she should start putting a note on the front door when Piper was napping. Or would that be a bit too cranky?

Stacey opened the door and saw Colton on the porch. Her heart took a huge dip.

Colton removed his Stetson. "We need to talk."

Chapter Six

"I'm sorry. I shouldn't have taken advantage of you," Colton said.

Stacey felt her face heat with embarrassment and cringed. "Oh, no, I'm sorry. I shouldn't have interfered. I was supposed to be helping you with your girlfriend and ended up kissing you. I knew you had plans with her, but you and I got close and I stopped thinking about your girlfriend. I was just thinking about you and—"

"Stop," he said, and took her mouth in a kiss, then pulled back. "There is no girlfriend."

She stared at him in confusion. "No girlfriend?"

"No girlfriend," he repeated. "There is no one else I can think about right now. You're the only woman on my mind," he said.

Floored, Stacey could only gape at him. "I don't know what to say."

"You don't have to say anything. Just know that I didn't want to take advantage of you," he said and walked away.

Stacey gawked after him, wishing she could produce some magic words, but her tongue wouldn't even form basic syllables. "Colton," she finally managed, but he was already in his truck.

She was at a pure loss. He'd given her no chance to respond. How could she tell him how she really felt? How could she let him think their kiss was totally his fault? She raced to the back of the house and found her mother in between phone calls.

"Piper's asleep. Do you mind watching her for a while?" she asked.

"Not at all," her mother said. "Is there a problem?"

"I just need to go somewhere," she said, and didn't want to hang around long enough for her mother to question her further. Her mother was extremely intuitive. Stacey grabbed her purse, pulled on her coat and headed for her car. As she drove toward the Foster house, she tried to find the words to explain her feelings for Colton. She kept rehearsing several verbal scenarios, but none seemed adequate.

With no great plan in mind, she stomped up the steps to the Foster house and rapped on the door. A few seconds passed, and she knocked again.

The door whipped open and Colton looked at her. "What are you doing here?" he asked. "Listen, we don't have to talk about what happened again. I know you don't think of me that way," he said. "In a romantic way."

"Stop telling me what I think," Stacey said. She didn't know any other way to express her feelings for Colton except for kissing him, so that's what she did. She pulled him against her and kissed him as if her life depended on it.

Colton couldn't help but respond. He wrapped his arms around her and drew her to him. He clearly couldn't resist her. "You feel so good," he muttered. "Taste so good," he said, sliding his tongue past her lips.

Stacey felt herself heating up way too quickly. She wriggled against him, wanting to feel every bit of him. She wanted his skin against hers. She slid her hands up to the top of his head and continued to exchange open mouth kisses with him.

"I want you so much," she whispered.

"What do you want, Stacey?" he muttered.

"All of you. I want all of you," she said, her need escalating with each passing moment.

Colton's hands traveled to forbidden places. Her breasts and her read end. Beneath his touch, she felt herself swell like a sensual flower.

"Are you sure about this?" Colton asked, teasing her nipples to taut expectation.

"Yes, yes," she said, clawing at his chest. "I want you so much."

"Then you're gonna get me," he muttered and

pulled her up into his arms and carried her down the hallway. He took her into his bedroom and set her down on his bed.

"You're sure?" he asked a second time.

"More than sure," she said, and whipped off her shirt and bra. "Are you?" she asked, daring him.

One, two, three heartbeats vibrated through her, and Colton began to devour her with his hands and mouth. She had never felt such passion in her life. He made every inch of her body burn with desire and need for him. Stacey hadn't felt this alive in months…or ever.

She kissed his chest and belly…and lower. He groaned and took her with the same hunger.

"You taste so good," he said.

"So do you," she said, and pressed her mouth against his in a fully sexual kiss.

"I want to be inside you," he said, his tone desperate.

"I want you the same way," she said.

He pulled some protection from his bedside table, and finally, he pushed her legs apart and thrust inside her.

Stacey gasped.

"What?" he asked.

"You're just—" she said and broke off.

"I'm just what?" he asked, poised over her.

She took a deep breath and laughed breathlessly. "Big. You're big."

He shot her a sexy smile. "I'll try to make that work for you," he said, and began to move inside her.

They moved in a primitive rhythm that sent her twisting and climbing toward some new high she'd never experienced. She continued to slide against him, staring into his dark, sexy eyes.

When had Colton become so desirable to her? What did it matter? she asked herself and threw herself into making love to him. Stacey clung to his strong shoulders, and with every thrust, he took her higher and higher.

"You feel so good," he muttered. "So good."

Stacey felt herself clench and tremble. A climax wracked through her. She could hardly breathe from the strength of it.

Seconds later, she felt him follow after her, thrusting and stretching in a peak that clearly took him over the edge. He clutched her to him and gasped for breath.

Stacey clung to him with all her might. "Two words," she whispered. "Oh, wow."

He rolled over and pulled her on top of him. "When did you turn into the sexiest woman alive?"

Stacey laughed. "Me?"

"Yeah, you," he said, and kissed her again.

She sifted her fingers through his hair, enjoying every sensation that rippled through her. She loved the feeling of his skin against hers, his hard muscles. She slid her legs between his and savored his hard thighs. His lips were unbelievably sensual.

"I'm not sure how this happened," she said.

"Neither am I," he said. "But I'm glad it did."

They made love again until they were breathless. She wrapped her arms around him, shocked by how he'd made her feel. Stacey was in perfect bliss.

After that second time, Colton looked down at Stacey, all warm, sexy and satisfied in his bed, and felt a triple shot of terror. What the hell had he done? He hadn't just kissed his sister's best friend. He'd made love to her. Twice.

He held her tightly against him but was horrified by what he had done. "You're an amazing woman."

"You're a flatterer, but I'll take it," she said, cuddling against him.

"This is great, but I don't want us to have to make excuses to my family," he said.

A sliver of self-consciousness slid through her eyes. "Oh, good point," she said and bit her lip. She moved off of him, and he immediately regretted the absence of her body and sweetness.

Stacey quickly pulled on her clothes. "I should leave."

"Let me walk you to your car," he said, still full of questions and regrets. He pulled on his jeans and shirt.

Stacey grabbed her coat that had been left on the foyer floor. "I'm glad your mother didn't discover that," she said.

"We're talking about building a separate house, soon," he said.

"I understand the need for privacy," she said. "I don't have it. But I'm lucky to be able to live with my parents."

"I feel as if I should drive you home," he said, still upset with himself and overwhelmed by his feelings.

"I'm okay," she said, but she looked uncertain. The mood between them suddenly seemed awkward.

"Are you sure?" he asked.

She pressed her lips together in a closed-mouth smile. "Yes, I am," she said and shrugged. "I guess I'll see you around."

"Right." He nodded, thinking they had moved way too fast. Stacey had big responsibilities, and he might not be the right man to help her with them. He hadn't considered his previous experience with Piper a rousing success. "We'll talk later," he said, and helped her into her car.

"Yeah," she said, but didn't meet his gaze. She started her car and tore out of his driveway faster than a race car. He wondered if she regretted going to bed with him. He couldn't blame her. His parents' ranch wasn't exactly the most romantic environment.

Colton struggled with his own emotions over what they'd just done. They were friends, weren't they? If that was true, why had he wanted her so much? Why did he still want her? Whatever was happening between him and Stacey was complicated as hell.

* * *

Stacey forced herself not to look in her rearview mirror as she pulled away from the Foster ranch. She had clearly lost her mind, rushing back to tell Colton that she wanted him, too. Even though he'd said she'd been on his mind, it wasn't as if he'd said he wanted her in a forever way. She'd better not forget that. She'd been through a similar situation with Joe, although he'd given her an engagement ring. With Colton, he'd made no promises. He'd just taken what she'd eagerly offered, but afterward the expression on his face had been one of discomfort.

Buyer's remorse, she thought. He'd taken the goods, but now he wasn't sure he wanted them.

Pain twisted through her. She felt like a fool. Why had she believed Colton was different? She was all too familiar with this scenario. She'd been through it and lived to regret it during the past year of her life. When would she learn? she castigated herself. When would she stop throwing herself at men only to learn they only wanted her for a little while? Not forever. She wondered if she and Colton had just made a big mistake.

How could they go back to being friends now? Was that what he wanted? Humiliation flamed so hot it was as if a hole burned in her stomach. She pulled to a stop in front of her parents' home and shook her head at herself.

Glancing in the mirror, she saw that her hair was a mess, her lipstick smudged halfway across her face.

If her mother caught sight of her, she would know that Stacey hadn't just been running errands. Jeanne Fortune Jones was one of the most intuitive women on the earth, especially when it came to her children.

Stacey searched through her purse and found an elastic band but no brush. She raked her fingers through her hair and pulled it into the low messy bun she frequently wore. She pulled out a tissue and wiped the gloss off her face, then reapplied just a little to her lips. She checked the buttons on her coat, making sure they were properly fastened.

Holding her breath, she decided to make a dash through the foyer. "Well, there you are," her mother said from the kitchen. "I was starting to wonder where you'd gone so long."

"Sorry, Mom," Stacey said, pulling at the buttons on her coat. "I've got to use the bathroom or I'm going to burst. I'll be out in just a few," she said, and ran down the hall. She took her time, then hid out in her bedroom a little longer.

"Stacey, dinner's ready," her mother called.

Stacey cringed, then stiffened her spine. She could and should focus on Piper. As she stepped into the kitchen, she was relieved to see her brothers Liam and Jude sitting down to the table along with her father and mother. Her father and her brothers were too busy talking about the ranch to notice her. Her mother had put Piper in her high chair. As soon as Piper spotted Stacey, she lifted her hands and smiled in joy.

Even though the baby wasn't speaking yet, her nonverbal language soothed Stacey's heart, and she immediately picked up her baby. "Well, hello to you, Sweet Pea," she said, and sat down with Piper in her lap.

"She's never going to learn to be happy in her high chair if you don't leave her in there," Jeanne said.

"I'll put her in her seat in a couple minutes. How could I resist that smile?" Stacey asked.

"Your food will get cold," her mother warned.

Stacey shrugged. "I'm not that hungry."

Her brother Liam glanced at her. "In that case, I'll take Stacey's share."

Her mother shook her head. "You will not," she said. "Besides, there's plenty to go around. Stacey made this meat loaf yesterday, so she deserves a few bites."

"I hope you didn't mind putting it in the oven," Stacey said, rising to get some dry cereal for Piper.

"Not at all. You were just gone longer than I expected, so I started getting a little worried," she said, and Stacey felt the unasked question in her mother's voice.

She sighed, knowing she would have to fib, and heaven knew she wasn't any good at deception. "I ordered something for Piper, and I wanted to see if it had been delivered to the P.O. box yet. No luck, and there was a long line at the post office," she said. Part of her tale was true. She *had* ordered something for Piper, but it wasn't due for days. "Then I stopped by to visit Rachel, but she wasn't there. She had saved a recipe for homemade baby food I thought I might try. I guess the whole trip was a washout. Was Piper okay while I was gone?" Stacey sprinkled some cereal on the top of Piper's high chair, then set her child in the seat.

"An angel. She took a long nap and woke up in a quiet mood," her mother said, and finally took a bite of her own food. Her mother was usually the last to eat. "You need to sit down and eat," she told Stacey.

"I am," Stacey said and took her seat. She forced herself to take a bite.

"Did you happen to see Colton when you stopped by the Fosters'?" her mother asked as she took a sip of coffee.

Stacey's bite of meat loaf hung in her throat, and she coughed repeatedly.

"What's wrong with you? Are you choking?" her brother Jude asked, then thumped her on her back.

"Water," her mother said, standing up and leaning over the table to pick up Stacey's glass of water and press it into Stacey's hand.

Stacey took a few sips. Everyone looked at her expectantly. "Sorry," she said sheepishly. "I think I tried to breathe the meat loaf instead of eat it."

Liam chuckled. "Make sure you teach that little one over there a different technique."

"I will, smarty-pants," she said, and was determined to take the focus off herself. "The Winter Festival is right around the corner. I can't decide whether to bake apple/blueberry pies, chocolate pies or red velvet cupcakes."

"Apple/blueberry," her father said.

"Chocolate," Liam said.

"All three," Jude said.

Her mother laughed. "Aren't you glad you asked their opinions? Any of those sound good to me, but make sure you bake an extra one of whatever you end up making for us, or there's going to be a lot of complaining," Jeanne said, tilting her head toward her husband and sons.

Stacey smiled in relief. She would escape an inquisition this time.

The next few days, Stacey developed a plan for her tutoring service. She knew her strengths were math and science, so she decided to focus on those subjects as she contacted the local schools. She also sent an email to Rachel since she knew her friend was doing her student teaching this semester.

Her mother caught her reviewing a flyer at the kitchen table and gave a sound of surprise. "When did you decide to start tutoring?"

"I've been thinking about it for a while. Piper is older, but still manageable. I'm hoping to schedule the sessions during after-school hours. She takes a long afternoon nap, so I'd like to take advantage of that time and bring in a little bit of money."

Her mother frowned. "If you needed money, you

should have asked for it. Your father and I are happy to help you," she said, squeezing Stacey's shoulder.

Stacey's heart swelled at her mother's support. "You and Dad are already letting me stay here without paying rent. I don't like feeling as if I'm not contributing." She sighed. "I don't like feeling like a deadbeat."

Her mother sat down beside her. "Oh, sweetheart, you're no deadbeat. You fix the meals and do the laundry and cleaning here. For goodness' sakes, I barely have to lift a finger with all you do."

"Thanks, but—"

"No buts," Jeanne said. "We know that Joe hasn't offered any financial support, and he should have. At some point, you may have to confront him about that."

Stacey shook her head. "I hate the thought of it. He rejected both of us so thoroughly. I hate the thought of asking him for anything."

"But he *is* your baby's father," her mother said. "He has some responsibilities."

"I wish he wasn't Piper's father. I wish her father was someone more responsible, mature. Someone who adored her." A lump of emotion caught in her throat. "I wish—" she said, her voice breaking. She took a deep breath. "It doesn't matter what I wish. I'm probably never going to find anyone that loves me and Piper, and I need to stop whining about it. Piper and I are so blessed that my family loves us and supports us."

"Well, of course we love you," her mother said.

"But you're young, and you have a long life ahead of you. You'll find someone—"

"I don't think so," Stacey interrupted. "I can't count on that. I can't hope for it. I've just got to focus on doing the right thing for Piper, and I think tutoring is the right thing."

"If you're sure," her mother said. "And you know I'm happy to babysit for Piper anytime you need."

"Thank you, but I'm hoping I can do this while she's napping," Stacey said.

Her mother studied her for a long moment. "I worry that you don't get out with people your age very much. You and Rachel see each other now and then, but not that often. I wondered if you and Colton might be getting friendly."

"Oh, no. He was just trying to be nice and brotherly," she said, although her teeth ground together when she said it.

"If you say so," her mother said. "There's no reason you two can't enjoy each other as friends."

"Hmm. We'll see," Stacey said in a noncommittal voice. "At the moment, I need to make some copies of these posters and call in some favors from my teacher friends."

"All right. You sound like a busy girl. Are you still going to make desserts for the Winter Festival?" her mother asked.

"That's next week and I've already got it on my calendar," Stacey said. "I've got it under control."

Stacey did her best to stay busy during the next

days. She didn't want to think about Colton. She couldn't help feeling dumped. Thank goodness, no one except she and Colton knew what had happened between them. The longer the time passed, the more she knew, for certain, that now that he'd indulged his passion for her, he was done with her. She would have felt a bit more used if she didn't recall how much pleasure she'd experienced with him. Every once in a while, a stray image crossed her mind of the way he'd felt in her arms, the way he'd kissed and caressed her. Every time she had one of those thoughts she wanted to stomp it from her mind the same way she would stomp a spider. This was not the time for her to be thinking about her sexual needs.

Darn Colton Foster. Ever since Joe had abandoned her, Stacey had buried all her interest in sex. It hadn't been that difficult. But being around Colton had brought those emotions back to life, and these feelings were not convenient.

Not at all.

"Colton, I need you to take my pies to Dessert Booth number three-B at the Winter Festival tomorrow," Olive Foster said when he walked into the kitchen late Thursday evening.

Colton shook his head. "I've got a mile-long list of chores I have to do tomorrow. Maybe Rachel can do it."

"Rachel is student teaching. She can't do both,"

his mother said. "You'll only have to be there three hours."

"Three hours," he echoed, incredulous. "Why can't I just drop them off?"

"Because they need people to help work the booth," she said. "And I'm volunteering to help the handicapped at the festival."

"You may need to help Dad if he decides to do any of the chores I have planned for tomorrow," Colton grumbled.

His mother shot him a sharp look. "That's a terrible thing to say about your father."

"You know he has a problem with his back, even though he won't admit it," he said.

She sighed. "I'll guilt him into coming with me. That should keep him out of trouble."

"Kinda like you're guilting me into working a bake sale?" he returned.

"Colton, you are bordering on being disrespectful. What's wrong with you lately, anyway? You've been as grumbly as a bear with a sore paw. Are you having girl trouble?"

"Oh, for Pete's sake." Colton lifted his hand. This was not a conversation he wanted to have with his *mother*. "Just stop, Mom. I'll do the darn bake sale." Hell, he would do ten bake sales as long as he never had to discuss this subject with his mother again.

After lunch, the following day, Colton loaded up his truck with his mother's apple pies and drove to the Winter Festival. There was already a mile-long line of people waiting to get inside, but since he was a so-called vendor, he walked right in. It took him a while, but he finally found his assigned booth. He set the pies on the card table and turned around to get the second batch.

He was in such a hurry he nearly walked straight into someone just outside the booth.

"Don't," she said, and *she* sounded remarkably like Stacey. He should know since he'd been hearing her voice in his dreams every night. "Don't knock over the cupcakes," she said.

Colton grabbed two of the boxes that threatened to fall off the tower of desserts she carried and noticed Stacey was hauling Piper on her back at the same time she carried the desserts. "For Pete's sake, what are you doing?"

"I brought cupcakes and pies. I couldn't decide which to bake, so I made both," she said, striding toward the same booth where he just set down his mother's apple pies. Stacey frowned, then looked up at Colton. "What are you doing here?"

"My mother guilted me into bringing her pies and working this booth," he said.

"Well, that's just great," Stacey said, clearly disgusted. "Just great."

"Hey, my mother pushed me into this," he said. "Don't blame me."

"I'm not blaming you for bringing your mother's pies," she said, but he could hear she hadn't finished her sentence. There was more to it.

"You're blaming me for something," he said. "I can hear it in your voice."

"I'm blaming you for not calling me, Colton Foster. That was pretty rotten, unless you just wanted me for a quick roll in the hay," she said, and turned away from him.

Chapter Seven

Colton thought about responding to Stacey, but he couldn't find the right words. So he returned to his truck, swearing all the way as he hauled in the second load of pies. How could he explain himself? He wanted her, but he wanted to be sensible. With her history, he thought they should take their time. Plus, there was a baby involved. He didn't want to mess things up.

"Hey, Colton, you sure you don't want to share one of those pies with us while we wait out here in the cold?" a neighbor called from the crowd.

Colton paused only a half beat. "I don't have a fork handy for you," he said in return.

"I don't need a fork. I'll just eat with my hands. I love your mama's pies," the neighbor called back.

Colton chuckled despite his black mood and shook his head, walking to the dessert booth he would share with Stacey. His chuckle faded as he reentered the booth and set down the second haul of pies.

"You might want to put those on the table against the wall," she said as she arranged the desserts on the front table. "We don't want them to know we have a lot of them. They'll buy faster if they're afraid we'll run out."

"True," he said, and moved half the pies to the back table. "Are the cupcakes okay?"

"The frosting on two of them got smashed, but the rest are okay," she said.

"I can eat the damaged ones," he offered.

She shot him a disapproving glance. "We may have someone desperate enough to buy them," she said. "We're trying to make money for the mobile library, not stuff our faces."

"I wasn't suggesting we stuff *our* faces," Colton said. "I just wanted to stuff *mine*."

Stacey rolled her eyes and turned away, but Piper craned her head around to look at him. He couldn't deny she was cute. She batted her big eyes at him. Colton hid his face in a game of silent peekaboo.

After a few times of peekaboo, Piper let out a gurgling laugh. It was, Colton thought, one of the best sounds in the world. He played peekaboo again, and Piper let out a joyous shriek.

Stacey whipped around and glared at him. "What are you doing?"

"Nothing," he said. "Nothing."

"Hmm," she said in a short, disbelieving tone. "The attendees should be coming through soon." She turned her back to him again.

Piper looked at Colton, and he wiggled his fingers and smiled at her. She smiled coyly, then giggled.

Stacey glanced over her shoulder at Colton.

"What?" he asked.

She made a huffing sound and turned away to arrange a display of cupcakes. Colton couldn't help noticing Stacey's backside. He couldn't help remembering squeezing her curvy hips as he slid inside....

Colton felt his body instantly respond to the memory and visual. He shifted his stance and cleared his throat. "How have you been doing?"

Stacey immediately whipped around and stared at him with a wide-eyed gaze. "Since when?"

Colton shrugged. "Since last week."

"Oh, you mean since the day we had sex twice in your bed and you rushed me out the door because you didn't want your family asking questions and then chose not to call me. Even once."

Colton's gut twisted. Just in case he'd wondered, he now knew that Stacey had wanted him to call. He'd been unsure about how she'd felt since he'd taken her in his bed. Before, during and afterward, he'd wished that he could take her somewhere more private, but he'd been so hungry for her, and she'd seemed to feel the same way about him. Someone had to get control in this situation, although he was pretty sure he was nowhere near control. He didn't know if he could trust Stacey's feelings for him. To be honest, he wasn't sure if he was a rebound man for her.

"I wasn't sure you wanted me to call," he admitted.

She screwed up her face in a confused expression. "Why would you think that?"

"Well, you left pretty fast," he said.

"After you pushed me along," she said.

"I was trying to protect you," he said. "Did you really want to have to explain to anyone in my family why you were walking out of my bedroom with your hair all messed up and your coat on the floor in the hallway?"

Her hostility lowered a couple of notches. "I guess not," she said and paused. "But that still doesn't explain why you haven't called," she practically spat at him and turned around as the first attendees began to wander toward their booth.

After that, everything turned into a blur. It seemed that everyone who stopped at the booth wanted a pie or cupcake. The cupcakes went first because they were pretty and inexpensive. Every time Colton sold one of those cupcakes, he had to resist the urge to eat it. Red velvet with cream cheese frosting. His mouth watered. He kept hoping he could persuade Stacey to give him one of the defective cupcakes, but they were moving so quickly that he was losing hope. The booth was so tight she brushed against him every time she moved from the front to the back. He didn't know which was worse, the temptation of Stacey's body or of her red velvet cupcakes. Another brush of her sexy hips against his and his question was answered. He wanted Stacey a lot more than he wanted cupcakes.

"I need to ask a favor of you," she said, pulling at the straps of her baby carrier.

He shrugged. "What do you need?"

"To go to the bathroom. I'd prefer to go without Piper. Can you take her for a bit?" she asked.

"Sure," he said, feeling lame for not offering sooner. "Can I have one of those cupcakes in exchange? Half?" he added when he saw her frown. He needed some sort of consolation for how much he wanted her and couldn't have her, although he suspected a cupcake wasn't going to do the job.

"Half," she said, and eased the carrier from her shoulders. "You want to put her on your back?" she asked.

"That sounds good," he said, and turned around so she could help strap the carrier on him.

"I'll put her so she's facing away from you. That way she'll keep her fingers out of your hair. I'll be back soon," she said.

"We'll be here," he said.

Piper made an indistinguishable noise, but she didn't cry, so he figured he was good. He continued to sell pies and cupcakes, although the cupcakes were growing scarcer. "I need to put this cupcake in a protective place," he murmured and hid the treat behind his cup of coffee at the back table.

He smelled a peculiar odor, but was too busy to focus on it when a rush of attendees bought pies. Thank goodness, the pies were popular. Colton couldn't deny, however, that he was ready for this to be over. He'd rather be driving posts in dry ground than this.

Stacey returned, appearing breathless. "Sorry. The restroom was on the other side, and there was a line."

"There is always a line for the ladies room," he muttered and turned his back so Stacey could help disengage him from Piper.

"Oh, no," she said. "Oh, no."

"What's wrong?" he asked. "Is she okay? She's been quiet for a while."

"That's because she fell asleep," Stacey said.

"And that's bad because?" he asked.

"That's not the bad part," Stacey said. "Piper pooped all over your back."

"Oh, great," he muttered. Now he understood the source of the strange odor. "I'm glad someone feels better."

Colton and Stacey shut down the booth until the next volunteers were scheduled to appear. They were mostly sold out, anyway. Stacey helped Colton out of the baby holster, and she took Piper to the restroom while Colton headed home. This was one of the rare instances that Colton didn't have a fresh shirt in his car, so he drove with his windows open due to Piper's stink bomb.

He headed straight for the shower, stuffed the shirt in the washer on rinse, then fixed himself a bowl of soup from the Crock-Pot on the kitchen counter. Colton parked himself in a chair in the den to watch an action movie. He wanted to think about anything except Stacey and Piper, and it wasn't just because Piper had cut loose on him. He had been trying to dodge his feelings for Stacey since they'd been together, and seeing her today had felt like a slap in the face. Even though he saw his orderly life veering out of control when he was with her, he'd missed her terribly, and now he didn't know what to do.

A knock sounded, and Colton rose from his chair and opened the door. Stacey stood on the front porch holding a small covered plate. "I'm really sorry about what happened with Piper. It doesn't happen that often, but, well, babies can be messy. I kept back a couple of the cupcakes for you. I hope you'll accept them along with my apology."

His chest tightened at the kind gesture. "That was nice of you," he said. "Would you like to come in?"

She bit her lip. "I have Piper in the car."

He hesitated. "Bring her in. There's chicken noodle soup in the Crock-Pot. I'm just watching a movie."

"Are you sure?" she asked, her gaze searching his.

"Yeah, I'm sure," he said.

Stacey returned to the car and pulled Piper from

her car seat, along with a diaper bag. Colton rushed to take the bag for her. He wouldn't admit it aloud, but he was still a little gun-shy with the baby.

Stacey pulled a blanket from the diaper bag and spread it on the floor in the den while Colton ladled soup into a bowl for her and poured a glass of water. Colton returned to find the baby propped against some kind of pillow thing that kept her from falling over.

"Does she like that?" he asked.

"She can actually sit by herself, but she eventually topples. She didn't get much of a nap today, so I thought she could use a break," she said, and placed a couple of toys next to the tot. "I'm hoping for an early night."

"I'll say," he said, and set Stacey's soup on a tray on the end table.

"Thanks," she said, taking a seat on the sofa. She took a spoonful of soup. "This is good. It's nice eating someone else's food for a change."

"Yes, it is. That's probably why my mother does most of the cooking. She's good at it, so we just let her do it," he said.

"My brothers don't cook either. I got more interested in cooking when I went to nursing school," she said. "Then, after I got engaged, I wanted to take my mother's recipes with me when I got married. But that didn't work out," she said, and took another spoonful of soup.

An uncomfortable silence stretched between them.

"I'm sorry I didn't call," he finally admitted. "I wanted to." How could he tell Stacey that he feared he was a rebound man for her?

She looked up at him in surprise. "You did?"

"Of course I did," he said. "I didn't exactly hide how I felt with you when you were in my bed."

She looked away. "Well, I have a previous experience with someone who wanted to go to bed with me, but then left."

His gut clenched. "I don't want you to feel that way, but it just seemed as if everything was moving fast. It was out of control."

She nodded. "I wanted you, but I didn't want to want you."

"Exactly. I wasn't ready for what I was feeling," he said.

She gave another slow nod and took another sip of her soup. "Does that mean you want to forget what we did and go back to being friends?"

"That might be like trying to put the toothpaste back in the tube," he said. "I always want to be your friend, but I'd be lying if I said I don't want to be more."

Stacey met his gaze. "Then what do you want to do about it?"

The sexy challenge in her green eyes felt like a velvet punch in his gut. "Maybe we could spend some more time together. Go to Vicker's Corners, see a movie, take some walks when it's not freezing. Go for hot chocolate," he said, and wondered if she would find his suggestions lame.

She gave a slow smile. "That sounds nice, but people are gonna talk. I'm used to gossip, but you're not."

"I can handle it," he said defensively, although Colton had never liked people getting in his business. "I'm just probably not as nice about it as you are," he said and chuckled.

At that moment, he heard his parents walk through the front door. "Yoo-hoo," his mother called. "We're home."

Piper, who had been surprisingly quiet, looked up from playing with her toy.

Colton's mother and father came to a dead stop as they glanced into the den. "Hello, Mr. and Mrs. Foster," she said, rising from the sofa. Colton also rose. "I stopped by with a few of my red velvet cupcakes, and Colton offered me some of your delicious soup."

"Good for both of you. I'm glad Colton showed you some hospitality. Frank and I heard there was a mishap with the baby at the winter festival today, but couldn't get the details."

Stacey chuckled. "I'll let Colton fill you in on that. I should be getting Piper home."

"I'll just say I'll wash the shirt I wore today twice," he said.

His father gave a nod. "Been there, done that. It's good to see you and the baby, Stacey. I hope you don't mind if I get some of that soup."

"Not at all," Stacey said.

"Oops. Sounds as if there might have been a little mess," Colton's mother said. "Don't rush off," she said as Stacey put away Piper's baby paraphernalia. "Let me see that sweet little munchkin. She's growing like a weed."

Mrs. Foster extended her arms to the baby and smiled when Stacey handed Piper to her. "What a friendly little sweetheart. Your mother says she's sleeping through the night most of the time."

"That's right. We had a rough time the first few months, and she still has her moments. But don't we all?" Stacey said.

"I can tell you're a good mother. I always knew you would be. You just seem to roll with whatever comes your way. I know Rachel is going to be upset that she didn't get to see you and the baby," Mrs. Foster said. "Are you sure you can't stay?"

"I really should go," Stacey said. "I'm hoping for an early night. It's good to see you."

"Same here," his mother said, then plopped the baby in Colton's arms. "Here. You carry Piper out to the car. Stacey could probably use a little break from hauling around this little chunk of love after today."

Colton automatically stiffened but soldiered up. He couldn't disagree with his mother. After his limited experience with Piper, he was surprised Stacey wasn't exhausted all the time. From what he could tell, branding an entire herd of cattle would be easier than watching over a baby.

He carried Piper to the car and let Stacey fasten her into her safety seat. Piper fussed a little at the confinement. "You just better get used to this," Stacey said in a kind but matter-of-fact voice. "You'll be sitting in a safety seat every time you get in the car." She shook a toy connected to the front of the seat to distract the baby, and Piper quieted down.

"You're good with her. I'll say that much. She can be a handful," he said, shaking his head.

"She's curious and sweet, but you're right. She has her moments," Stacey said.

"That's when those bubbles come in handy," he said.

Stacey stared at him and smiled. "So you *did* use the bubbles that night you kept her for me?"

"Hey, I had to hit the ground running. That diaper bag is like a bag of tricks," he said.

"You almost sound as if you're still afraid of her," Stacey said. "My little Piper couldn't terrify a big, strong man like you, could she?"

"Of course not," he lied because the baby did have the ability to scare him more than a fright movie. "I'm just no baby expert like you are."

"Maybe she'll grow on you," Stacey said softly.

"Maybe," he said. Piper's mother was growing on him. He leaned toward Stacey and took her mouth in a lingering, sweet kiss that made something inside him fill up and want more at the same time. "I'm glad you came over. I'll call you."

"I'm going to be really upset if you don't," she warned.

He liked hearing that bit of testiness in her voice. It made him think she wanted him, too. "No problem," he said and kissed her again. He pulled back. "You're habit-forming."

"That's good to hear," she said. "I think your mother is watching from behind the curtains in the front room. She may ask questions. That's what mothers do."

"That's okay. I have the perfect answer," he said, putting his index finger under her chin.

"What's that?"

"Nunya. Nunya business," he said, and her laughter made it worth the inquisition he knew he would face when he went inside the house.

That night, Stacey slept better than she had in months, partly because Piper slept long and hard, and partly because being with Colton just made her feel better about life. He didn't have to do much. Just his presence made her feel calmer and more optimistic. She didn't want to overthink his effect on her. Stacey just wanted to enjoy it.

He called her on her cell the next morning, and she could tell he was outside and the wind was blowing. "Good mornin'," he said.

"Good morning to you. How long have you been out and about?" she asked as she toted Piper around the kitchen.

"Since a couple hours ago. You know the routine. I have to get up early in order the get the heavy chores done so my father doesn't hurt his back," he said.

"I wish you could talk him into seeing the doctor," she said. "It's as if he's in complete denial of this health problem."

"You're exactly right. He's in denial until he ends up in bed for a few days. Then he takes it slow. A few weeks after that, he thinks it'll never happen again. But enough of my crankiness. How would you like to go into town and get a burger at the grill? Early dinner?"

"That sounds like fun, but my parents are going to be at the winter festival all day, so I would have to bring Piper," she said. When he didn't immediately respond, she filled the gap of silence. "We can go another time. We don't have to go today."

"No," he said. "Let's take her with us. What time will work?"

"I'd like to get her back on schedule with her afternoon nap. Is four-thirty okay?"

"Sure. I'll pick you two ladies up at four-thirty. See you then," he said and disconnected the call.

Stacey felt a spurt of excitement and danced around the room with Piper. "We have a date."

She spent the morning entertaining Piper, then ran laundry and cooked a big pot of chili in the afternoon. She changed her clothes three times and might have changed them once more if Piper hadn't awakened. Her brother Jude must have smelled the chili from miles away because he stomped into the house an hour after she'd put it on the stove. Her brothers were at the family dinner table more often than not, despite the fact that they had their own places to live.

"Thank goodness there's food," he said. "I'm starving." He looked at Stacey and Piper and gave a double take. "You two look as if you're headed someplace special," he said.

Stacey resisted the urge to squirm. "Just going to the grill with a friend," she said.

"Rachel?" he asked as he grabbed a bowl from the cabinet.

She shook her head. "Nope. Do you mind setting that Crock-Pot on low and putting the lid on it if you leave before Mom and Dad get home? I think they should be here within a half hour," she said.

"Sure," he said and grabbed a spoon. "Any crackers or bread?"

"Crackers are in the cupboard." A knock sounded at the door, and her heart leaped with silly excitement. "Gotta go."

"Hey, you never said who is going with you to the grill," he said.

"That's right," she said, unable to stifle a little giggle. "I didn't. See you later," she said, and ran to the door and threw it open.

"Hi," she said, thinking it was ridiculous to be so excited about going to the grill in town. This proved the point that she really needed to get out more often.

"Hi to you and Miss Piper," he said. "You're both looking beautiful. You ready to go?"

"Thank you, and we are," she said.

"I'll carry Piper to the truck. I see you have the magic tricks bag," he said, gingerly taking the baby in his arms.

"It goes wherever Piper goes," she said. "Listen, do you mind if we take my car? I've already got the safety seat, and it'll be easier to keep it in there than switch it from my car to yours again."

"Good plan," he said. "It didn't occur to me."

"Probably because you haven't spent a lot of time with babies," she said.

"My mistake," Colton said. "The education of Colton Foster continues. I'll let you fasten her into that contraption," he said after he carefully set Piper into the seat.

As usual, Piper complained about the confinement, and Stacey distracted her. Within a couple moments the baby calmed.

"Have you ever tried to take her on a road trip?" he asked.

"Not unless you call the hour drive to Lubbock a road trip," she said. "She's really not a bad rider, but I wonder if she might get fed up with it after several hours. I have visions of throwing everything but the kitchen sink into the backseat to keep her amused."

"I think my parents must have done that when we took a trip to Dallas one time, although my Dad wouldn't put up with any foolishness when we got older."

"My father is the same way, maybe even more so," she said. "Deke Jones is a stand-up guy, but I have to admit that he didn't join me for any tea parties when I was a little girl. He was too busy for that."

"It's funny the things we remember. My mother showed up for most of my basketball games, but my father only came to a few each season. I always knew they both loved me, and that's what's important," he said.

"Very true," she said. "Now that I've had Piper, though, I find myself wishing she had everything I had growing up and more."

"Like what?" he asked.

"She has some of it," Stacey said. "A safe, warm home and family who love her, but—" She broke off, feeling self-conscious.

"But what?"

"Nothing," she said, feeling her face grow warm with embarrassment. "You'll think I'm crazy."

"No. I won't. Tell me."

Stacey smiled and shook her head. "I'm hoping I can talk one of her uncles into having a couple tea parties with her," she said. "I think it's good for little girls to have good men who are involved in their lives."

"I'm sure you're right about that," he said. "What do little girls eat at tea parties, anyway? I can't believe they like tea."

"Juice and cookies," she said.

"That's not all that bad," he said.

"No. It's the little chairs and pretending that makes it tough for a grown man," she said.

"Which of your brothers have you targeted for this?" he asked.

"I have a year or two before the parties will begin," Stacey said. "But I'm thinking Toby would be a natural. He's already a foster father. If not him, I may be able to con Jude into the job, especially if Piper serves something I've made."

"Sounds as if you're planning ahead," he said.

"Once I had Piper, I couldn't just think about the moment anymore. I had to think about the future, too."

"Is that why you seem sad sometimes?" he asked.

Stacey looked at him in surprise. "You think I seem sad?"

"Well, different. You used to seem happier," he said.

She thought about that for a moment. "I worry more," she confessed as he pulled into the small parking lot for The Horseback Hollow Grill.

He cut the engine and turned to her. "No worrying for the next couple of hours," he told her. "After all, you're about to eat a gourmet meal with the handsomest guy in Horseback Hollow," he joked.

Stacey smiled. The gourmet meal was a stretch,

but she was beginning to think that Colton was the best man in Horseback Hollow. She wondered why she'd never noticed until now.

Chapter Eight

"Oooh, what a cute baby," the server at The Grill said, then glanced at Stacey and Colton. "What a good-looking family. I bet you hear that all the time. I'm Maureen, and I'm new here in Horseback Hollow." Her gaze returned to Piper. "Look at that chin," she said, tickling it. "Just like Daddy's. Now, what can I get for you today?"

"Burger loaded and hot chocolate," Colton said. "What about you?" he asked Stacey.

"Grilled cheese and hot chocolate. Extra marshmallows please," she added.

"Will do," Maureen said and turned away.

"Sorry about that," Stacey said.

"Sorry about what?" he asked.

"That the waitress said Piper looked like you," she

said, feeling extremely awkward. She didn't want Colton to feel pushed into a relationship with either herself or Piper.

"She said we have the same chin," he said, rubbing his own chin and glancing at Piper. "I just didn't know I already had two."

Relief raced through her, and she swatted at him. "Stop that. She clearly only has one chin, but there's no denying those chipmunk cheeks. She looks as if she's packing a load of acorns." Stacey rubbed her daughter's cheek. "But you're gorgeous, anyway," she said.

"She is. She looks like you. Minus the chipmunk cheeks," he said.

"I'll take that as a compliment," Stacey said, and Maureen returned with their hot chocolate.

"Anything else I can get you?" she asked.

Colton glanced at Stacey. "We're good," she said.

Their food was served just moments later, and Stacey relished her grilled cheese sandwich. Although Piper was well-fortified with cereal on her high-chair tray, she watched every bite that Stacey took.

"She's getting more interested in food," Stacey said. "Especially whatever I'm eating."

"Can't blame her. What does she get? Dry cereal? She looks as if she wants to reach right over and grab the rest of your sandwich. You're clearly starving her."

"Right," Stacey said, shooting him a mock chastising look. "This is probably more than you want to know, but she's allowed to have strained and pureed fruits, vegetables and meats."

Colton made a face. "I didn't hear hamburger on that list."

"She doesn't have any teeth. She'd have to gum it," Stacey said.

A woman stopped by their table. "Why, Stacey Jones. I haven't seen you in ages."

Stacey recognized the woman as a member of her church. Stacey had missed quite a few Sundays since Piper had been born. Truth be told, she'd missed more than she'd attended since she'd gotten pregnant. "Mrs. Gordon, it's good to see you. How is your family?" Stacey asked as she stood and gave the woman a hug.

"We're hanging in there. My husband has had a terrible time with gout, but we keep plugging. Look at your baby. She's just gorgeous," Mrs. Gordon said, and glanced at Colton in confusion. "Colton Foster, right? For some reason, I thought your fiancé's name was Joe."

Stacey's stomach knotted. "He was. Joe moved to Dallas. But Piper is thriving, as you can see."

"Yes, she is. And how nice for both of you to have big, strong Colton around," Mrs. Gordon said in a coy voice.

"Hmm," Stacey said, so ready for the woman to move along. "Thank you for stopping by," she said. "And please give your husband my best."

She sank back onto her seat. "Why does everyone have to know everything about everyone around here?" she muttered and took a sip of her hot chocolate. She wondered how long she would be answering questions about Joe and why they weren't together. At this point, it looked like forever.

After they finished their meal, Colton drove Stacey and Piper back to Stacey's house. "You're awfully quiet," he said.

"I know I said that we have to expect people to talk here in Horseback Hollow because that's what they do, but I hate having to talk about Joe. People always look at me with pity. Poor Stacey. She couldn't keep her man," she said.

"Joe's leaving wasn't your fault. He couldn't handle the responsibility of a baby. He's the loser in this situation, not you," he said. "If you need another way of looking at it, aren't you glad that you and Piper aren't stuck with a man who doesn't love you? You deserve better than that."

"When he first left, I was in shock. I couldn't believe he would abandon his own child and me. It made me wonder if I ever really knew him," she said.

"Do you wish he would come back and the two of you could get back together?" Colton asked.

"I did for a while," she confessed. "It sounded like the perfect ending to a fairy tale that had gotten off track. But I don't know that I would ever be able to trust him again. I do know that I'm not the same woman who fell for him years ago. I just wish he wouldn't have rejected Piper. That's the worst part," she said.

Colton pulled the car to a stop in the Joneses' driveway. He leaned toward her. "I'm not sure this little outing cheered you up all that much."

She blinked at him. "I didn't know that was the purpose," she said. "I thought we just wanted to spend some time together. We did that with no meltdowns from Piper, and I had terrific hot chocolate and company."

"You're some kind of woman, Stacey, and don't you forget it," he said as he lowered his mouth to take hers in a delicious kiss.

Stacey felt her heart race. Her body immediately responded. His kiss triggered all sorts of forbidden emotions and sensations. She slid her hands beneath his jacket to pull him closer. He responded by nearly hauling her onto his lap.

"Damn this console," he muttered and kissed her again. He slid one of his hands from her waist upward to her breast.

Her nipples turned hard, and she felt her need for him pool in all her secret places. "Oh, Colton," she whispered and scrubbed at his chest, wishing she could feel his naked skin.

His kiss turned hot with want and need, and she strained toward him, her body and mind recalling how good he'd felt inside her. She wanted him that way again. Now.

The sound of Piper gurgling and talking her baby

language penetrated past the mist of arousal crowding her mind. Colton froze. Stacey did the same.

Frustration nicked through her. "This is hard," she said.

"In more ways than one," Colton said, his voice taut with forced denial. "Between you living with your parents and me living at the ranch, I feel like a randy teenager," he said and pulled back.

Stacey felt the same sense of dissatisfaction she heard in his voice. "What do you usually do? How do you usually handle things when you and a woman—" She broke off, wondering if she really wanted to know about Colton's previous partners.

"That's part of the reason I want a place of my own," Colton said. "Privacy. But I've felt as if I needed to keep an eye on my father, and I haven't wanted to tell my parents I want to build. The time is coming sooner than later, though. In the past, the women had their own places or we spent the night in Vicker's Corners."

"A whole night?" she echoed. "I'm trying to imagine spending the whole night away from home without a lot of questions." She sighed. "I wish this were easier."

He kissed her lightly on the mouth as if he didn't want to get anything started between them again. "Most good things don't come easy. Let me walk you and Piper to the door."

Stacey said good-night to Colton and walked

through the door. No sooner had she closed the door behind her than her brother Jude appeared.

"So, you went out with Colton again? Are you sure that's a good idea?"

Taken aback by his confrontational manner, she tilted her head at him. "I enjoyed Colton's company, a grilled cheese sandwich and hot chocolate. Is there anything wrong with that?"

"Well, not really," Jude said.

"We had a chaperone. Nothing naughty happened. Trust me, nothing naughty *can* happen," she grumbled.

"I just want you to be careful. I don't want to see you get hurt like you did with Joe," he said.

"Colton is nothing like Joe. Nothing," she said, and took Piper to the nursery. It was true that Colton was nothing like Joe, but Colton had never asked her to marry him. Stacey felt a stab of concern that Colton wasn't interested in being anybody's baby daddy, which also meant he wouldn't want to be Piper's daddy.

That night when she went to bed, it took her a long time to fall asleep.

Colton did a last check around the north pasture, then returned to the house. Grabbing a cup of decaf, he sank onto one of the recliners in the den. He halfway watched a basketball game through his drooping eyes. Feeling himself drift for a few moments, he awakened when his father walked into the room and got into the other recliner.

"Hey," Colton said.

His father nodded.

"You worn out from the second day of the winter festival?" Colton asked.

His father gave a heavy sigh. "Your mother insists on staying for the whole thing, and she wants me to stay with her."

"Your back okay?" Colton asked.

"A little sore. Nothing unusual," his dad said.

"Any time you want to go for lunch in Vicker's Corners, I'm glad to take you. There's a chiropractor there," he said.

"Chiropractor?" his father said. "Don't they crack your bones and put you in traction? Sounds as if that would make you worse."

"They make adjustments," Colton said. "They help get your back in alignment."

"Hmmph," his father said in disbelief. "Well, that's not why I came in here. Your mother wants me to talk to you."

"About what?" Colton asked, feeling curious and studying his father.

His father sighed. "It's about Stacey and her baby."

Colton frowned. "What about them?"

"Well, it's not really any of our business," his father began, and Colton immediately knew this wasn't a discussion he wanted to have with his father.

His father cleared his throat, obviously uncomfortable. "You need to be careful with Stacey," he said. "After what Joe did, she doesn't need anyone taking advantage of her."

Indignation rolled through him, and he pushed the recliner into the upright position. "I wouldn't take advantage of Stacey. What makes you think I would?"

"Well, you look as if you're getting, uh, friendly with her," he said. "I mean you look as if you want to be more than friends," he said, then rubbed his face with his hand. "Oh, for Pete's sake. Just treat her right. That's all I'm gonna say."

Colton met his father's gaze. "I'll treat her right. You and Mom don't need to worry."

"Good," his father said. "I'm glad that's over. Who's playing tonight, anyway?"

"The Bulls and Lakers," he said.

His father nodded. "Looks like a close game."

Colton didn't respond. His mind was too busy with his father's remarks. He resented the interference. He was a grown man. Colton stood. "I'm gonna hit the sack," he said. "Good night."

Colton headed down the hall and was intercepted by his sister, Rachel. In no mood for anyone else's comments, he lifted his hand. "Don't say a word," he said.

She frowned at him. "About what?"

"About Stacey and me," he said.

Her eyes widened in surprise. "Stacey and you?" she echoed. "What's going on? I've been crazy busy and haven't had a chance to talk with her for several days."

"Never mind," he said, and headed for his wing of the ranch.

Rachel bobbed along behind him. "Are you two seeing each other? That would be so cool," she said. "As long as you don't hurt her. You have to swear you won't hurt her, but I love the idea. I'll call her right now."

"She's got a little baby," Colton said. "She might be in bed trying to get some sleep."

Rachel's face fell. "True. Well, give me the scoop. When did this happen?"

"Rachel," he said as gently as he could, "it's none of your business."

The next morning, Stacey awakened with a different sense about herself and her life. She realized that in many ways she'd been hiding from the world, ashamed of how her relationship with Joe had ended, embarrassed that she and Piper had been dumped by him. The whole situation had made her feel like that mathematical expression *less than*.

She was ready to start reclaiming her life. Taking a quick shower and getting dressed, she fed Piper and dressed her in a cute outfit with stockings. She met her parents just as they were headed out the door to church.

Her mother looked at her in surprise. "Where are

you two going looking so spiffy? Is there a mother/baby beauty contest I haven't heard about?"

Stacey laughed in pleasure at the sweet way her mother had voiced her curiosity. "Piper and I are going to church this morning."

"Oh, my." Her mother covered her mouth and sniffed. "I've been waiting for this day."

"I hadn't turned into a total heathen," Stacey said.

"Oh, no. Not that," her mother said. "I'm just so proud of you and Piper. I want everyone to see what a good job you're doing with her. I think you will be an inspiration to many people."

"I don't know how inspiring I'll be if she starts screaming in church," Stacey muttered. "But I think it's time."

"Yes, it's time," her father said impatiently and pointed at his watch. "If we don't get moving we'll be late."

"You can sit with us," her mother said as they were hustled out of the house. "I'll be happy to take Piper out if she gets fussy."

"I'll take her out," her father said. "Especially if she starts fussing before the offertory."

"Deke," her mother said in disapproval. "Shame on you."

"What? I'm just being a nice granddaddy," he said and chuckled. He helped Jeanne into his truck, and Stacey tucked Piper into the car seat in her Toyota, then followed her parents to church.

She felt a twinge of nostalgia as she walked into

the small chapel her family had attended since before she was born. She'd celebrated so many holidays and Sundays in this place. As soon as she walked inside with Piper in her arms, she saw several familiar faces. She waved at each of her neighbors, then took her seat with her parents.

Piper did well until the minister began to speak. She got a little squirmy, but Stacey couldn't blame her. There'd been plenty of times she had gotten fidgety when a minister spoke. Despite her squirminess, Piper didn't let out a peep until the congregation sang a benediction.

"Good job," she said, praising the baby, and left the pew. Several people greeted her and made a fuss over Piper. There was no mention of Joe, but Stacey was prepared in case someone did. She made her way to the back of the church and found Rachel waiting for her with open arms.

"I decided to come to church at the last minute today. I'm so glad I did. Look at you and Miss Piper," she said, squeezing the baby's hand. "All dressed up for church. She must have done well during the service. I didn't hear her."

"She, ahem, *sang* during the benediction," Stacey said.

Rachel giggled. "Good for her. She'll be in the choir before you know it. Listen, I'm sorry I haven't been in touch with you. Changing careers to education and doing my student teaching has made me crazy. I had no idea how much time the lesson plans and parent meetings would take."

"No worries," Stacey said. "I know you've been busy."

"Not so busy that I should be the last to know that you are dating my brother," Rachel said.

Stacey groaned. "Oh, no. Not you, too. It seems as if everyone has an opinion about us seeing each other. And it's not as if either of us has any privacy where we live."

Rachel raised her eyebrows. "Privacy?" she echoed. "You want privacy with my brother?"

Stacey shook her head and waved her hand. "Forget I said anything."

"You sound like Colton," Rachel said. "He didn't want to talk about it either."

"Well, who wants to talk about a relationship when it's first starting? Who knows where this will go? Colton has a lot on his mind with your father's back problem. He keeps trying to talk your dad into seeing a doctor, but your father won't go. Colton says he's got to stay one step ahead of your dad to keep him from hurting himself."

Rachel nodded. "My father avoids doctors at nearly all cost."

"I think Colton wonders if you might be more successful with your father than he has been," Stacey said, hoping she'd managed to distract Rachel from her questions. "I need to get Piper home to change and feed her, so I need to head out to my car."

Rachel tagged along. "Well, just so you know, I'm all for this. Colton is a great guy, and you're the best friend I could ever have. He would be lucky to get you, and in a way, maybe you would be lucky to get him, too. Especially after Joe," she said.

"I don't want my relationship with Colton to have anything to do with Joe," Stacey said as she buckled the baby into her car seat. "I want to leave that behind."

"Kinda hard to do when Joe is Piper's father," Rachel said.

"He's been invisible for over a year. I need to move on," she said.

Rachel met her gaze and nodded. "Good for you. But when it comes to my brother, you need to know something," she said and lowered her voice. "He's slow at making the moves, so you may have to help him along."

Stacey bit her lip to keep from laughing at Rachel's warning. She couldn't help thinking of the scorching lovemaking she'd experienced with Colton. "I'll keep that in mind," she managed.

"Good," Rachel said. "I'll call you soon. Maybe I could babysit for you sometime."

"You may have a hard time squeezing me in with your student teaching," Stacey said.

"Maybe," Rachel conceded and gave Stacey a hug. "But I have three reasons to try to make that happen."

"Three?" Stacey said, hugging her in return.

"My brother, you and me. Wouldn't it be cool if you were both my best friend and sister-in-law?"

The possibility gave Stacey a jolt. "Oh, Rachel, don't go there. These are very early days."

"Well, it's not as if you haven't known each other forever."

"Yes, but I haven't always had a baby. I'm not at all sure Colton is ready to be a father to a child that isn't really his."

"He might need a little persuading, but I think it could be done." Rachel shivered. "It's too cold for me out here. I'll call you."

Stacey watched Rachel race to her car and tried to unhear the words she'd just heard, but it was like trying to unring a bell. What if she and Colton got married? Was it even a possibility? Her heart squeezed tight with a myriad of emotions. She closed her eyes and shook her head. She shouldn't even think about it.

The next day, Colton went into town to get some equipment to repair some fences and overheard a couple of workers talking about something happening at the bar.

"So, what's going on?" he asked.

"*Live* music at the Two Moon Saloon on Tuesday," the worker said.

"Really? I can't remember the last time there was live music at the bar," Colton mused.

"And I hear there might be dancing," the worker said. "I'm taking my girlfriend."

"Hmm," Colton said. He wondered if Stacey would be able to go on such short notice. On the way home, he called and left a message about the live music and continued on with his chores.

Stacey must have returned his call while he was out fixing a fence. Her mom would keep Piper. She sounded excited. He hoped that whoever was performing didn't bomb. The smile he heard in Stacey's voice did strange things to his gut. He felt a little lighter, a little less burdened as he pulled into the driveway to his house. His conversation with his father had kept him awake for an extra hour last night, but Colton knew he wanted to spend time with Stacey and she felt the same way about him. He knew his mother and father shouldn't be involved in this decision, and if they intervened again, he would have to speak his piece.

Colton stomped up the steps to the house with the winter wind whistling through his coat. He was dog-tired and all he wanted was a home-cooked meal. If that wasn't available, he would heat some canned soup and make a sandwich.

"Hiya," Rachel called as he passed the den. She appeared to be doing lesson plans or grading papers.

"How's it going?" he asked.

"I wish I'd earned my first degree in education. This is so time-consuming," she said.

"I'm not sure it changes much, sis," he said. "I

never hear teachers talking about how much extra time they have."

"True, I guess," she said. "But I like it, so maybe I won't notice the time."

He nodded. "I'm gonna get whatever is available in the kitchen."

"Wait," she said, scrambling to her feet. "I talked to Stacey at church yesterday," she said.

"Great," he said and moved toward the kitchen.

"I also talked to her today. Amazing what I can learn about my brother from his girlfriend," she said, following him.

He shot her a quelling glance.

"What I mean is I didn't realize how bad Dad's back is. Stacey said you've offered to take him to Vicker's Corners to see a doctor, but he won't do it," she said.

"That's right," he said, opening the fridge and hoping to find something wonderful. He spotted a small bowl of leftover beef stew and snatched it up.

"She also said that you thought Dad would be more likely to go with me to Vicker's Corners to see a doctor."

"Right again," he said. He put the stew in the microwave, then pulled some sliced ham, cheese and bread out of the fridge and went to the counter. "The trouble is you'd have to trick him."

Rachel frowned. "What do you mean?"

"You would need to make an appointment with him and find some other reason for him to go. You'd take him to lunch, then take him to a doctor's appointment and beg for forgiveness afterward. He would forgive you within twenty-four hours, less if he got some relief from his back pain."

Rachel's frown deepened. "That sounds like a lot of trickery," she said.

"As if you haven't done the same ten times over for less honorable reasons," he returned as he slapped the meat and cheese on the bread and slathered it with Dijon mustard.

"I wish Dad would be more reasonable about medical treatment," she muttered, crossing her arms over her chest.

"You and me both," he said, when the microwave beeped. He grabbed his bowl of stew and sandwich. He would worry about water later.

Rachel poured a glass of ice water and sat down at the kitchen table. She put the glass at the place opposite from her. "Well, sit down," she said, waving her hand. "We have to figure out exactly when and how I'll do this trickery."

"Dad is a sucker for his little girl. Just invite him to go to lunch with you, then take him to a doctor afterward," Colton said.

"Stacey and I didn't just talk about Dad," Rachel said.

A bite of sandwich lodged in Colton's throat. He coughed repeatedly and washed it down with a gulp of water. "Oh, really," he said in a deliberately noncommittal tone.

"Yes," Rachel said. "Stacey said the two of you could use some privacy. What do you say about that?"

"Privacy begins at home," Colton said.

Rachel made a face at him. "I'm trying to help."

"Then stay out of it," he said. "There's a baby involved. I don't want to be responsible for messing up that child's life. I'm taking it slow or not at all."

Chapter Nine

Colton sat across from Stacey in the Two Moon Saloon while a trio played. They might not win any awards, but folks got up to dance every now and then.

"This is fun," she said as she took a sip of her mixed drink.

Colton had smuggled in some cranberry juice for her to mix with vodka and ice. He'd known the bar wouldn't keep much juice on hand. If they did, their supply would quickly deplete on a busy night like tonight, with more women asking for mixed drinks instead of beer or straight liquor. It appeared many Horseback Hollow men had viewed the live music at the bar as a good date-night opportunity, so more women took part in drinks with their men.

"I'm glad you like it," he said, taking a long swallow from his beer.

"You don't like the group?" she asked.

"I like them fine," he said. "It's nice to hear some live music here for a change."

"I agree," she said, and the trio began to play a slow song. "Any chance you would dance with me?"

"Sure," he said, his body tightening at the sexy expression in her eyes.

Colton led her onto the tiny dance floor and pulled her against him. "You feel good," he whispered into her ear.

"You feel good, too," she said, and stretched her body so that it molded against his.

Colton couldn't help wishing they were both naked. Stacey was so sweet and inviting. He couldn't resist her. With every beat of the song, he felt the gentle friction of her feminine body against his. He grew harder with each touch.

She lifted her head, and it was the most natural thing in the world for him to take her mouth. She slid her sweet, silky tongue in his mouth, and his internal temperature turned hotter and hotter. He couldn't help but return her kiss.

His heart slamming against his chest, he squeezed her against him, and she stroked his jaw. The music ended, but he didn't want to release her.

She breathed against his throat, and it was all he could do not to lead her out of the bar and take her in his truck. He took a deep breath to pull himself under control. "I guess we should sit down now," he said in a low voice.

"I guess we should," she said, looking up at him with wanting for him in her eyes. "But that's not what I want."

"Me neither," he said. "It stinks."

She gave a slow smile that sizzled with sexuality. "Yes, it does," she said and pulled back.

Colton prayed that his arousal would calm down. He still wanted her, but his mind knew this wasn't the place or the time. They returned to the table and he took a drink of his beer while she took a sip of her cocktail.

She met his gaze with an alluring smile. "This makes me feel young again. Lately, I've been feeling kinda old and tired."

"You need to give yourself a break. Piper's got that kick of Fortune Jones in her. She's going to let you know when she wants something, and she'll try to make you race to get it for her."

Stacey lifted her eyebrows in surprise and took a sip of water. "What makes you say that? Are you implying that she's spoiled?"

"Not at all," Colton said. "I'm just saying she's— assertive. Isn't that what everyone is supposed to be these days?"

Stacey pressed her lips together, then let out a big laugh that filled him all the way up inside. "That sounds mighty close to calling my baby a brat."

"She's not a brat," Colton said. "Not yet."

Her eyebrows flew up to her hairline. "Not yet?" she echoed.

"Right," he said. "She's not even walking. She won't turn bratty until she's three."

Stacey gave a slow nod. "Good to know."

"Do you really disagree?" he asked.

"I just hope I do this parenting thing right. I don't want to be too harsh or too permissive. It's not as easy as it looks," she said.

"You're doing great," he said, and put his hand over hers.

"Thanks," she said, and her smile made his gut do strange things.

"Well, well," a male voice said. "A new couple. What would Joe say?"

Colton glanced up to see Billy Hall, Joe's best friend, sneering at Stacey and him.

"Hey, Billy. How are you doing?" Colton asked as politely as he could manage.

"I'm doing great. I just wonder what Joe would think if he found out one of his groomsmen was kissing his ex," Billy said.

"Joe is history," Stacey said. "He hasn't been around for over a year."

Billy pursed his lips. "Oooh, that's harsh. He might not like that."

"How would you know?" Colton asked.

"We talk every now and then," Billy said.

"You ever tell him what a useless piece he was to leave Stacey and his child?"

Billy gave an awkward shrug. "Well, no. He's my friend. I couldn't call him names." Billy paused. "But I could tell him his ex was taking revenge on him by getting involved with one of his best friends. How you like those leftovers?"

Without a pause, Colton rose and shook Billy hard.

Stunned, Billy stumbled backward. "What the—"

"Don't insult Stacey again," Colton said, clenching and unclenching his fist. "Ever."

"Hey, I was just taking up for Joe," Billy said.

"He doesn't need you to take up for him. He's doing fine," Colton said. "He isn't getting up in the middle of the night to take care of a baby. He's not giving Stacey one dime of support."

Billy's eyes widened, and he lifted his hands. "Okay, okay. I get your message." He turned toward Stacey. "Sorry," he said and walked away, wiggling his shoulders as if he were trying to straighten out his spine.

His heart still slamming against his rib cage, he sat down and took another long sip of beer. "Sorry about that," he said.

She pulled his hands into hers. "That was very nice of you. Not necessary, but—"

"Very necessary," he said. "You don't deserve that. Joe's not here. He hasn't done anything to redeem himself in this situation."

She lifted his hand to her lips and kissed it. "I'm not thinking about Joe anymore."

Colton felt a dozen emotions slamming through him, but the way she kissed his fist made his heart turn over like a tumbleweed. "You deserve better."

"I'm getting better," she told him.

They finished their drinks, and Colton drove Stacey home. What he wanted was to bring her to his bed and make love to her, but that wasn't going to happen tonight. He stopped the car and she immediately unfastened her seat belt and pulled his face toward hers. She took his mouth in a kiss that blasted through him like a ball of fire. Sweet Stacey had somehow turned into a sexy tigress, and he was reaping the benefit.

She slid her hands over his chest down to his abdomen and lower. Colton was torn between telling her to stop and begging her to continue. At the same time, his hands moved of their own volition to her breasts. With her coat open, he tugged at her sweater and slid his hands upward.

She continued kissing him, devouring him with her delicious mouth. She reached to unbuckle his belt at the same time the floodlights spilled over the front yard of her parents' home.

"Whoa," he said, stilling her hands even though he was dying for her to continue. He could just imagine her mother or father coming out for a friendly chat.

"What? Why?" she asked, looking at him with such a sensual, needy gaze that he could hardly stand it.

"Lights came on," he said gently and pulled her into an embrace.

Stacey gave a low growl of frustration. "This is ridiculous. We're adults, not teenagers."

His heart slamming into his chest at what felt like a hundred miles an hour, he took a deep breath. "I'll figure something out."

She sighed, then leaned her forehead against his chest. "Pretty crazy. Who would have thought I would be taking a cold shower because my best friend's brother is making me too hot?"

"You were hot before I came around," he said.

"You didn't notice before," she reminded him.

"I wasn't supposed to notice," he told her, rubbing her soft cheek with his hand. "You belonged to somebody else," he said, thinking of Joe. Joe, who hadn't stood by her when he should have.

After her date with Colton, Stacey felt as if she had a little more bounce in her step. Although she was still juggling her household commitments and taking care of Piper, she was thrilled to book her first tutoring session on Thursday afternoon. A mom with an elementary-school-age boy named Frasier brought her son to the ranch for Stacey to work some magic on him by helping him with math.

Stacey injected as much enthusiasm into the session as possible, but Frasier seemed quite listless. At one point he even laid his head down on the kitchen table. Concerned that he might be sick, Stacey mentioned the boy's condition to his mother. She felt a little guilty accepting the money from Frasier's parent, but made a mental note to perhaps give him an extended or free session in the future.

As soon as the boy left, Piper awakened from her nap. Stacey changed the baby, then carried her into the kitchen. "What a good girl to sleep all the way through my tutoring session. You're the best, aren't you?" she said to Piper as she gave her daughter a bottle. Piper sucked down her bottle in no time, and Stacey patted her back to help counter air bubbles.

"There my girls are," her mother said as she entered the house with bags of groceries. "Let me help you with those," Stacey said and pulled out a quilt for Piper. "Looks like you bought out the store."

Her mother laughed. "This was my big trip. I went to Vicker's Corners. Of course, if you add in gas, it may be a wash. But the grocery store there has a much better selection, and the prices are a little better."

Stacey rushed to her mother's sedan to help bring in the rest of the bags of groceries. "I see that you picked up some baby formula and baby food. I can reimburse you for that since I had my first tutoring session," Stacey said proudly.

Her mother smiled at her. "I forgot about that. How did it go?"

"Okay, except I hope that little boy wasn't sick. He sure didn't act like he felt well. I hope it will go better next time," she said.

"Oh, dear," her mother said. "I've heard there are a couple things going around. One is a quick but nasty stomach virus. Make sure you wash your hands."

"Good point. And I'll wipe down the table," she said. Stacey cleaned her hands and the table and helped put the groceries away as quickly as possible. She knew Piper would be wanting some food. Sure enough, just as Stacey unloaded the last bag, Piper let out a squawk.

"You go ahead and get her. I can take care of the rest," Mama Jeanne said.

Stacey put the baby in her high chair and pulled out a jar of pureed green beans. "Yum, yum," Stacey said. "Green vegetables."

Not Piper's favorite, but she must have been hungry because she eagerly consumed the first few bites. "She looks like a little bird when she eats from the spoon."

"She'll be reaching for that spoon any time now, and every mealtime will turn into a mess. Mark my words," her mother said.

"No problem. I'll just need a washcloth or paper towel. Oh, I meant to tell you that Piper and I will be riding with Colton to the Rothwell wedding on Saturday. The Rothwells are lucky that the Jergens offered them the use of their heated barn for their reception. I'm sure that's why they were able to invite so many people."

"Seems as if you and Colton are spending more and more time together," her mother said.

Stacey hesitated, then glanced at her mother. "You may as well offer your opinion on it, since everyone else has."

"Well, I wouldn't dream of interfering," her mother said. "Colton is a fine, fine young man. I just hope you two won't rush into, well, the physical aspect of a relationship. After all, you have a young baby."

Stacey gaped at her mother. "Mama, do you really think I would turn around and get pregnant again?"

"We're a very fertile family," her mother said. "Colton is likely quite the virile male and—"

Stacey covered her ears. "I don't want to discuss this anymore," she said. "It's not like Colton and I have lots of opportunities, between him living at his parents' house and me living at mine. Add in a baby and, oh, my gosh—"

"It's not that I don't approve of Colton because I very much do," her mother continued as if Stacey hadn't spoken. "I just don't want you to get into a situation where—"

"Stop," Stacey said. "Stop, stop, stop. Please."

Her mother pressed her lips together. "I like Colton," her mother said. "I like him better than I ever liked Joe. Your father does, too."

"Did you run into anyone interesting at the store?" Stacey asked because she had to change the subject, and it seemed that her mother knew everyone within a thirty-mile radius.

"As a matter of fact I did," her mother said. "Laurel Fortune was buying avocados in the produce department when I was there. She's such a sweet girl. Gave me a hug right away. I asked her how married life was, and she said the married part was great, but that she and Sawyer are very upset about the recent accident at their flight school."

"Oh, that's right. Did she say how Orlando is doing?" Stacey asked.

"He's still in the hospital, but they think he will recover. It may take a long time. She said how thankful she and Sawyer were that you were able to come and help stabilize Orlando until the paramedics arrived."

"I was glad I could help, but I was very concerned when I left," Stacey said.

"Don't dare tell anyone, but Laurel confided in me that the investigation has just started, but she and Sawyer are worried that it may not have been an accident."

Stacey gasped. "Oh, no. That would have been horrible. She thinks someone may have deliberately done something to cause the crash?"

"They don't know, but they're suspicious. Not everyone is happy about Fortunes coming to Horseback Hollow," her mother said, a worried expression on her face.

"Oh, that's ridiculous. It's not as if the Fortunes

are trying to take over the whole town. And why would they? They're all about making money, and there's not that much money to be made in Horseback Hollow."

"The Fortunes aren't all about money," her mother corrected her. "They've made the best from their opportunities and profited from them. Don't forget they are very active in charitable causes." Her mother took a breath. "And there's the fact that my brother James tried to give me a huge sum of money, although I probably shouldn't bring that up because the whole subject can get some people worked up."

Stacey couldn't help thinking of her brother Chris, who was still upset that her mother hadn't accepted the Fortune money; but she didn't say it aloud because she didn't want to add to her mother's misery.

"Stacey, are you angry that I turned down that money?" her mother asked in a quiet voice.

Surprised that her mother would ask her, Stacey shook her head. "You did what you thought was right. Do I wish I had the financial assurance to make sure that Piper will always have what she needs? Sure, but I know I can take care of that. Maybe not right now, but I'll make it happen. In the meantime, Piper and I both have something much more important than money. We have your love and support, and that's worth far more than money."

Her mother sniffed and walked across the room to hug her daughter. Stacey closed her eyes at the sensation of her mother's loving arms around her.

This, more than anything, was what she wanted to be able to give Piper the rest of her life.

"It makes me so proud to know what a good heart and soul you have. It makes me feel as if your father and I did something right," Jeanne said.

"Mama, I can assure you that I'll make plenty of mistakes, but you gave me a good heart and a strong sense of right and wrong. I also appreciate the value of hard work. Piper and I will be fine," she said, thrilled because she was finally starting to believe it.

Colton put on his tie and jacket and took one last glance in the mirror. This would be his first planned, semiformal evening with Stacey and Piper. He wanted it to go as well as possible. He hoped Piper was in a good mood because that could make a big difference.

He strode toward the front door.

"Woo-hoo, you look great," his mother called.

Colton smiled and turned to meet her gaze. "Thanks, Mom. You look great yourself."

"Well, thank you, sweetheart," she said, and moved toward him to give him a kiss on his cheek. "You going to pick up Stacey and her baby?"

"I am," he said. "I'll see you at the wedding and reception."

"You look good," his mother said. "She's a lucky girl."

"Thanks," he said. *I'm a lucky guy.*

He drove to the Joneses' ranch and knocked on

the door. He waited a couple moments, and Stacey finally answered the door.

"Sorry," she said. "I haven't been feeling great, and it took extra time to get Piper ready. The great news is she seems to be in a good mood."

"I'm all for Piper being in a good mood," he said, and studied Stacey for a moment. "You look a little pale. Are you sure you want to go?"

"I'm sure," she said. "This will pass. I probably haven't had enough water. I've been busy all day long."

"If you're sure," he said.

"I'm sure," she said and smiled. "Let's go."

Colton helped Stacey and Piper into Stacey's car, then got behind the wheel. He drove down the driveway of the Joneses' ranch and turned onto the main road. Stacey's silence bothered him. He drove a few miles down the road.

"I need you to stop," Stacey said. "I feel sick."

Colton immediately pulled to the side of the road. Stacey stumbled out of the car and got sick on the side of the road. He wasn't sure if he should comfort her or leave her alone. After a few moments, she got back in the car.

"I'm sorry, but I don't think I should go to the wedding. I think I caught a stomach virus from the little boy I was tutoring. Please take me back home," she said, and leaned her head against the headrest.

"Right away," he said, and made a gentle U-turn in the middle of the road. He took a quick glance at her and saw that she was taking deep breaths. He pushed the button to lower the passenger window.

"Thank you," she said.

Colton pulled into the driveway and stopped in front of the house. Stacey flew out of the car. "I'm sorry. I'll get Piper in a couple minutes," she said, and raced through the front door of the house.

Colton sat in the car, staring after her. Piper squirmed and cooed. It wasn't an unhappy sound, just an acknowledgment that the car had stopped. He took a deep breath but didn't glance back at the baby. He suspected that if he looked at her, she might start squawking.

He waited two more minutes, but there was no sign of Stacey. Well, darn, he was going to have to take Princess Piper inside. Stepping out of the driver's seat, he turned to the backseat and searched for the release of the safety seat. Piper squirmed, but she didn't yell at him. He finally found it and pulled her into his arms. Slamming the door behind him, he trudged up the steps to the house and walked inside to complete silence in the house.

Hearing the flush of a commode from the back of the house, he walked farther inside. "Stacey?" he called, once, twice, but there was no answer.

Colton sighed and looked at Piper. "Looks like it's me and you kid," he said. He suddenly realized he'd left the magic bag in the car and returned to retrieve it. The second time Colton entered the house, he decided not to call out to Stacey. She was clearly ill. That left him with one task, taking care of Piper.

"So, how's your diaper? Can you give me a little warning if you're going to do a complete blowout?" he said. "I'll need a whole box of those wipe things."

Piper looked at him and lifted her finger to his mouth.

"Is that your way of saying shut up? I thought women wanted men to talk more," he said.

Piper made garbled baby language, but it wasn't fussy, so Colton had hope. "You know, this isn't that much different than talking with most women. Most of the time I don't understand what they're saying."

Piper continued with her baby talk.

"I wonder if you know what you're saying," he said. "I should probably check your diaper, even though I don't want to."

Colton gave a peek and a touch. "Just wet," he said, excited in a way that he could never explain to a bunch of guys at the bar. "No poo. I can do this," he said, and put her down on the sofa and changed her diaper.

"Time for a bottle?" he asked and pulled one out of the magic bag.

Piper reached for it. He sank down on the couch while she sucked down the formula. When she was finished, she looked as if she were in a stupor. He propped her up on his leg. She let out a belch that would rival that of a trucker's.

"Whoa, that was impressive," he said and patted her on the back.

Piper let out another loud, extremely unfeminine belch.

"Way to go," he said.

Piper looked up at him and gave him a milky smile. That smile melted his heart. She was a sweetheart. In some dark part of his mind, he couldn't help wondering how Joe could have left her. How could he give up the opportunity to be a father to this sweet little girl?

Chapter Ten

Piper spit up a little on his suit's pant leg. Colton bit his lip, remembering the blowout at the festival. *Could be worse,* he thought, and removed his coat and tie. If Piper ruined his shirt, he could wash it. The tie and coat were more problematic. He lifted her in his arms and walked around the kitchen.

Colton wanted to check on Stacey, but he also wanted to give her some privacy. He'd had a couple stomach viruses in his life, and all he'd wanted to do was lie on the bathroom floor and pray for relief.

Piper began to babble again. Colton was just thanking his lucky stars that the sounds she was making were happy ones. "So, who do you like better? Spurs or Mavericks?"

Colton carried Piper around for a half an hour. It

seemed the easiest way to keep her happy. She grew drowsy in his arms, though, and he didn't know if he should put her down for the night. Plus, he was worried about Stacey. He meandered down the hallway to Stacey's room.

"Hey, Stacey," he said and tapped at the door. "Are you okay?"

"No," she called. "My stomach has been inhabited by an alien, and it has turned itself inside out."

He swallowed a grin. It must be a good sign that she could joke. "Can I do anything for you?"

"Just make sure Piper is taken care of if I croak," she said.

His heart squeezed tight. "Don't joke about that," he said.

Silence stretched between them. "I'm not gonna croak," she said. "I'm just gonna wish I could croak."

"Are you sure I can't get anything for you? Water? Soda?" he asked.

"Maybe some soda," she said. "Clear soda," she clarified.

"Done," he said and went to the kitchen. Juggling Piper from one arm to the other, he searched the refrigerator and found a can of seltzer. He poured it into a glass with ice and took it back to her bedroom.

"Got the soda," he said, knocking at the door.

A moment later, the door opened, and Stacey looked up at him as she propped herself against the doorjamb. He could honestly say she looked like death warmed over. She was pale, and her eyes were red-rimmed. "I can only take a sip," she said, and reached out to take a tiny drink.

"Are you sure you don't need to go to the hospital in Lubbock?" he asked. "You look pretty bad."

"I'm in the worst part of the virus," she said. "I just need to stay hydrated. One sip at a time." She closed her eyes. "I need to lie down. Can you watch Piper a little longer?"

"Yes, I just need to know—"

"Thanks," she said and shut the door.

Colton looked at the door for a long moment, then looked at Piper. Her eyes moved in a slow blink. "You look very sleepy," he said. "But I don't want you to wake up in the middle of the night. Maybe a late-night snack?"

He returned to the den and pulled out the magic bag. Rifling through it, he found a jar of peaches. "Sound good?" he said to her.

She drooped against his shoulder. Colton opened the jar and fed her while she rested in his arms. It required far more coordination than it took to wrestle a calf and brand it.

Piper scarfed down the pureed peaches and let out a hearty burp. Colton figured a poop was coming any moment. He felt a sudden surge of warmth on his legs. "Wait, wait, wait," he said, and lifted her up before she ruined his suit pants.

He laid her down on a blanket and grabbed the whole container of wipes. "I can do this," he said to himself. "I've done it before." Colton opened Piper's diaper and winced. Quickly, he cleaned her up and fastened her new diaper only to have her refill it.

"Oh, Lord, help me," he muttered and started cleaning her up again. Sprinkling powder on her, he fastened yet another diaper on her. Taking the little girl in his arms, Colton tossed the two dirty diapers into the kitchen can and walked toward the nursery.

Rummaging around the room, he found a gown. With some trouble, Colton removed Piper's shoes, tights and dress, then pulled on the gown. She whined at him several times.

"Cut me some slack. I haven't done this before," he said. He caught sight of some booties and pulled them on her feet. "Comfy?" he asked.

She wiggled and stared up at him. He stared back at her for a long moment and felt as if he was seeing the beginning and ending of the earth in her eyes. He couldn't look away.

Piper wiggled again, and he shook his head. He must have imagined that strange feeling, he thought. He picked her up and paced around the room. After a few moments, he decided to try out the rocking chair. He rocked her for several moments, then set her down in her crib on her back.

Bracing himself for her cry, he held his breath and waited. Colton counted to one hundred. No sound from Piper. He almost couldn't believe it.

Leaving the room and carefully closing the door behind him, he glanced back at Stacey's room. He wondered if he should check on her. Lost in a quandary, he stared at her door.

"Is there a problem?" Stacey's mother asked.

Colton nearly jumped out of his skin. He'd been so focused on Stacey and Piper he hadn't heard Stacey's parents enter the house. "Stacey got sick on the way to the wedding," he whispered, not wanting to awaken Piper. "We came back, but she was too sick to take care of the baby. I looked after Piper, and she's fallen asleep."

"If there's one thing I know, it's not to wake a sleeping baby," Jeanne said.

Colton smiled. "I'm with you on that, but I'm a little worried about Stacey. Would you mind checking on her?"

Jeanne disappeared into Stacey's room for a moment, then returned to the hallway. "She's falling asleep as we speak. I think the worst of the virus is past. I feel bad that this was her first experience tutoring."

"Knowing her, she won't quit," Colton said.

"Very true," Jeanne said to him and squeezed his arm. "Thank you for looking out for Stacey and Piper tonight."

"Piper was a breeze," Colton said. "I just wish I could have helped Stacey a little more."

"You helped her by taking care of Piper." Jeanne gave him a considering glance. "Looks like Piper may be getting used to you."

"I think I just got lucky with her tonight," Colton

said. "I always feel as if I'm spinning the roulette wheel with that little one."

"Don't underestimate yourself," Jeanne said.

"If you say so," he said. "You sure you don't want me to hang around a little longer in case you need an extra set of hands?" he asked, feeling oddly reluctant to leave Stacey and Piper.

"I'll be fine," she said and chuckled. "I had to juggle babies when they were sick many times when my children were young."

"I guess so," he said, and felt a little foolish. Of course Jeanne Fortune Jones knew what she was doing. The woman had seven children, after all. "I'll head on home, then. Tell Stacey to give me a call when she's feeling better."

"I'll do that," her mother said. "Thank you again for looking after both of them."

He nodded and collected his tie, jacket and hat. "Good night," he said, and headed toward his truck. Colton had an odd, empty, gnawing sensation in his gut as he drove home. He should have been relieved to hand over the reins of Piper and Stacey's care to Jeanne, but he wasn't. Taking care of a temperamental baby while Stacey was sick? It should have been one of the most miserable evenings of his life. He should have run screaming the second Stacey's mom came home. Instead, he'd taken to the task quickly—and more easily than he'd imagined possible. And walking away from Piper—and her beautiful mother—was getting tougher by the day.

Something was wrong, very wrong. He needed to rethink all this.

Over the next couple of days, Colton brooded over his relationship with Stacey. With everyone else voicing an opinion about it, he needed to figure out his own thoughts. In a different situation, in a different—bigger, more crowded—town, he and Stacey could allow their relationship to develop naturally with little intervention. Since, however, both of them lived at home with their families, it seemed they were overwhelmed by prying eyes. Colton had feelings for Stacey and Piper, stronger feelings than he wanted to have at the moment, but he wasn't sure what he should do about those feelings—or what he wanted to do about them. Colton wanted to take things slow. He wanted to be careful. There was a baby involved, for Pete's sake. At the same time, he wanted so badly to be with Stacey and Piper. And yet he couldn't stop thinking about Joe. Why had he abandoned Stacey and Piper? How could he have? Colton had known that Joe's father hadn't been around much, but surely that wouldn't have prevented Joe from being the husband and father Stacey and Piper needed.

The quandary frustrated him so much that he worked outside until it turned dark. Maybe if he wore himself out, he would fall asleep without thinking about Stacey and Piper. He walked into the house with two goals in mind, a meal followed by a shower, but he caught sight of his sister Rachel grading papers in the den.

"Oh, there you are," she called out to him, jumping up from the sofa. "I thought you might have fallen in a hole."

"No, but I've been digging a few," he said, and continued to the kitchen. He foraged through the refrigerator and found some leftover baked chicken and rice. "How's life as a student teacher?"

"Busy, busy. But not so busy that I can't offer to babysit so you and Stacey can have an evening out by yourselves," she said, and shot him a cheeky grin.

"That's nice of you," he said and heated his leftovers in the microwave. "I'll have to check with Stacey when she's feeling better."

"Oh, she's feeling better," Rachel said. "I talked to her today. She hasn't called you yet because she's embarrassed that she got sick and you had to take care of Piper."

"I didn't mind taking care of Piper. I was glad to do what I could to help Stacey when she felt so bad," he said impatiently.

"What's wrong with you?" Rachel asked. "You seem grumpy."

"I'm just tired," he said, pulling a mug from the cabinet. "I've been up since the crack of dawn, working outside in this wind."

"Hmm," she said, crossing her arms over her

chest. "Are you sure it isn't anything about Stacey? You're not leading her on, are you?"

Frustration ripped through him, and he slammed the cabinet door. Swearing under his breath, he shook his head. "That's part of the problem," he said. "Everyone is watching every move Stacey and I make. Everyone feels the need to offer an opinion. Did you ever think we don't need your opinion? Did you ever think we don't want to hear what you think?" he challenged his sister.

Rachel drew back, her eyes widened in surprise. "Why are you so touchy? I just said you shouldn't lead her on. You know that, too."

"Then why did you feel the need to tell me?" he asked. The microwave dinged, signaling his food was ready. He poured himself a cup of decaf and took his dinner to the table.

"I just thought I should make sure," she said. "Stacey has been through a hard time. You know what happened with Joe."

"I do," he said. "You think I should stop seeing her?"

Rachel blinked. "Well, no. Why would you say that?"

"Because it's starting to look as if everyone either wants me to make a lifetime commitment right off the bat or pull back. Those are two extreme choices, considering we just started seeing each other. I've never dated a woman with a child before. I don't know if I'm ready to be an instant father. I don't know that much about kids, let alone babies."

Rachel sank onto the kitchen chair across from him and sighed. "This kinda stinks for you," she said. "Everyone is so excited for Stacey to get involved with a man who would be both a good husband and father that they're jumping to conclusions. Do you wish you hadn't started seeing her?"

"No. I *do* wish everyone would stay out of our business, but I don't see how that's going to happen. I have feelings for Stacey, and for Piper, too, but I have to figure out how to slow this down and get it more under control," he said.

Rachel nodded. "I know control has always been important to you, but good luck with it. I hear it doesn't always work in the romance department. My offer to babysit Piper sometime still stands. Otherwise, I'll let you figure this out on your own."

After eating his dinner and taking a hot shower, Colton went to bed, but he still didn't sleep well. He tossed and turned, trying to figure out what he should do about Stacey.

It was so cold that by afternoon the next day, he decided not to torture himself by staying outside any longer and chose to work in one of the barns close to the house. Hearing the barn door swing open, he turned to see Stacey standing in the doorway holding Piper in one hand and a basket in the other.

His gut took an involuntary dip at the sight of them. Both pairs of eyes were trained on him expectantly. "Hey there," Stacey said, and lifted her lips in a hesitant smile. "Have you recovered from taking care of us on Saturday night?"

"I think the more important question is whether you've recovered. How are *you* feeling?" he asked.

"Much better. It was a twenty-four hour virus. I've been holding my breath because I was afraid either you or Piper might catch it. You haven't felt sick, have you?"

"No, but I'm lucky that way. I don't get sick very often," he said, thinking he might not have gotten the stomach virus, but he still felt as if he'd caught some sort of emotional virus that was keeping him bothered and interrupting his sleep.

"I'm glad to hear that," she said. "I wanted to thank you. Seems like I'm doing that a lot lately," she said and smiled again. "I made some chocolate-chip cupcakes for you. You seemed to like the other ones."

She lifted the basket toward him, and he moved forward to take it. "You didn't have to do that, but thank you."

"My pleasure," she said, and the silence stretched between them. He felt her searching his face, but he couldn't offer her any answers if he didn't have any answers for himself.

She cleared her throat. "Well, I guess I'll go now. Thank you again for taking care of us on Saturday."

"I'm glad I could help," he said, and watched her walk out the barn door. Part of him screamed that he should go after her. But Colton had no clue what he would say.

* * *

Stacey walked away from the Fosters' barn with a lump in her throat. She couldn't bear to return to her house right away, so she drove into town and wandered around the Superette with Piper perched on her hip. Stacey knew she'd gotten her hopes up about Colton, and she clearly shouldn't have.

She picked up a couple bananas for Piper and seriously checked out the chocolate bars.

"Oh, no," a female voice said from behind her. "I'm counting on the hope that I won't crave chocolate once I deliver this baby. You're scaring me, Stacey."

Stacey turned around to find Ella Mae Jergens looking at the candy-bar display. She smiled at the pregnant woman. "I've always loved chocolate," she said. "Pregnancy didn't make it any worse, so don't base your fear on me."

"You're so sweet," Ella Mae said. "I really have to watch my weight. I'm married to an important man, and there will always be women chasing after him."

Stacey felt sorry for Ella Mae if she thought her husband would stray due to a little pregnancy weight. "I'm sure he adores you and sees you as truly beautiful."

Ella Mae smiled. "You've always been a nice girl. I was glad to hear you've been spending time with Colton Foster. Other people have been saying the only reason you got involved with Colton was to get back at Joe, but I didn't believe them. You ignore those rumors and hold your head high, Stacey. You deserve a good man."

Stacey's heart tightened with distress. "What other people have been saying that?" she asked. The only time she'd heard the horrible rumor was from Billy, Joe's friend.

"Oh, I don't know," Ella Mae said. "I heard it from my mother, who heard it from someone else. You know how this town is. Any kind of gossip, true or false, spreads like wildfire. Don't pay any attention to it. It will pass. But I will get just one candy bar," she said, and grabbed one from the display. "Here comes my mother. I'm spending the day with her. Take care, now," Ella Mae said, and headed for the checkout.

Sick from Ella Mae's comments, Stacey put the bananas back and fled the store. Could the day get any worse?

After Stacey returned home, she couldn't muster much conversation. Her mother tried to make small talk as the two baked side by side in the kitchen, but Stacey just wasn't in the mood. She wondered if having to take care of Piper on Saturday night had pushed Colton over the edge. Even though he'd always been sweet to the baby, he wasn't her birth father. He may have looked at his experience Saturday night and feared for his future.

Or had he heard more about the nasty rumor that Ella Mae had repeated to Stacey? Stacey knew that people in Horseback Hollow liked to gossip, but she was sick over the latest outright lie that was spreading like fire.

"You're very quiet, Stacey," her mother said as Stacey washed some pots and pans. "Are you feeling ill again?"

"No, no. I'm fine," she said, and dried the lid to a pot.

"Is something bothering you? I talked with your father last night about your financial concerns and he doesn't want you worrying," she said. "If you need more money—"

"I don't," Stacey said. "I got another student lined up for tutoring this week, but I know I'm not going to be making a lot of money right now. I'll figure that out later."

Her mother nodded and spread out a dish towel on the counter to dry. "Okay. Is there anything else on your mind? You know you can talk to me."

Stacey inhaled and sighed. "I'm not sure this thing with Colton is going to work out," she confessed and fought the urge to cry. She wiped the already clean counter for the third time.

"Why not?" her mother asked. "Did you decide you don't have feelings for him?"

"Oh, no," Stacey said, and swallowed her deep disappointment. "I have feelings for him, but I just don't think Colton is ready to be a daddy."

"Well, you could have fooled me. You should have seen how he hovered over Piper on Saturday night," her mother said with a firm nod of her head.

"That was just one night, Mama," she said. "He may be thinking he's not ready to take us on a full-time basis," Stacey said. "I can't really blame him. A lot of men wouldn't want to father someone else's child."

"You can't possibly believe that," her mother said. "Colton Foster is a good man. He would always do what's right."

"But how is it right for him to take on the responsibility for a child that isn't his?" Stacey countered. "How is it fair?"

Her mother frowned. "I think you may be jumping the gun. You need to give Colton a little time."

"I'm trying not to pressure him, but everyone we run into seems to want to make a comment or give advice about us seeing each other. I don't know," she said, shrugging even though she was miserable. "Plus, I haven't told you, but there's a terrible rumor going around about us. Some people seem to think that the only reason I've started spending time with Colton is to get back at Joe."

"Well, that's a complete fabrication. How would Joe even know that you're seeing Colton since he hasn't bothered to check on you or his baby?" her mother asked, indignantly. "If I were a lesser person, I could wish some bad things on that boy. Leaving you in the lurch like that. With a note, no less. Thinking about it still makes my blood boil."

Stacey knotted her fingers together, then pulled

them apart and knotted them again. "This is turning into a big mess. I think I'd better give Colton some space."

Jeanne Marie Fortune Jones stepped in line at the tiny Horseback Hollow post office. Her mind hopped and skipped to different issues weighing on her—Stacey's romantic predicament and her troubled son Christopher—as she patiently waited her turn.

"Hello, Jeanne. Good to see you," Olive Foster said as she got in line behind her neighbor. "How are you?"

"Good, thank you. I see you have packages," Jeanne said. "Christmas gifts you need to return?"

Olive nodded. "I overdid it this year, and my husband, Frank, can be so hard to please," she said with a heavy sigh. "What about you?"

"I'm sending a letter to my—" She broke off and smiled. "My sister in England, and another to my brother James. I know everyone uses email these days, but I thought both of them might enjoy a letter."

"That's nice of you. Are you still getting used to being a Fortune?" Olive asked.

Jeanne nodded and stepped forward. "It's still hard to believe, but it's wonderful having brothers and a sister and all these new nieces and nephews."

"I think it's so sweet that your children added the Fortune name," Olive said. "It shows a lot of family unity."

"Not all of them have," Jeanne said, thinking of Liam. "But they're all adults and it would be wrong for me to push them. They should make this decision on their own. It's not a perfect situation, but I'm glad most of them are interested in getting to know their new family." Jeanne thought, too, of her son Chris and the resentment he held against the Fortunes and their wealth. She wished he could let go of his ill feelings, because she knew he would be much happier if he did.

"How is Stacey doing? I heard she got sick the other night," Olive said.

"Yes, she did, but she's much better now. Colton took care of the baby during the worst part of it. You've raised a fine young man."

Olive beamed with pride. "Thank you. We're very blessed with both our children," she said.

Jeanne hesitated, wondering if she should say anything else. "I know that Stacey has enjoyed spending time with him lately."

"Yes, we are pleased about that. Stacey's a wonderful young lady."

Silence stretched for a long moment between them. "Of course, I understand if things don't work out. They've just started seeing each other, and we don't know what will happen in the long run."

Olive looked pensive and stepped closer to Jeanne. "It's none of my business, but is something wrong between them?" she asked in a lowered voice. "Colton hasn't said a word about her the past few days, and he seems a bit withdrawn."

"Well, I have to confess I've been concerned lately, too. Even though I love Colton, I told Stacey to be careful about getting involved again. She didn't seem to appreciate me giving my opinion," Jeanne said. "It's hard to hold your tongue when you worry about your children."

"I know what you're saying. I hate to admit it, but I asked my husband to speak to Colton about spending time with Stacey. I wanted it made clear that he shouldn't take advantage of her." Olive winced. "I wonder if I should have kept my thoughts to myself."

"They're adults and very responsible," Jeanne said. "I'd hate to think I helped to mess up anything by sticking my nose in their business."

"Me, too," Olive said miserably. "I suppose it wouldn't help to bring it up to Colton in casual conversation."

"Probably not," Jeanne said.

Olive sighed. "I guess we'll just have to do what we should have done from the beginning. Be quiet and hope for the best."

Jeanne nodded in agreement, but she worried about her daughter. Stacey had already been hurt enough. "Please don't tell anyone, but someone has started a terrible rumor," she confided to Olive.

"About Stacey and Colton?" Olive asked in surprise.

"Yes. Someone, and we don't know who, has been

saying that the only reason Stacey has been spending time with Colton was to get back at Joe because he left her. The reason I'm telling you is because I want you to know that is absolutely not true. I think Stacey has fallen for your son, but she feels as if she needs to back off and give him some breathing room."

Olive frowned and shook her head. "Why is it that people find it necessary to gossip about people who are just trying to do their best? If someone is stupid enough to repeat that rumor to me, I'll set them straight. You can count on it."

Jeanne felt a surge of gratitude inside her at Olive's protectiveness of Stacey. "You've always been the best neighbors we could have. I would love it if we could be in-laws," Jeanne said. "I'll be saying my prayers and crossing my fingers that our children will work this out."

Chapter Eleven

Piper had lost her favorite binky. Or, *someone* had lost Piper's favorite pacifier. Perhaps her father's hunting dog had eaten it. The who didn't matter. The fact was that Stacey needed to get a replica of the favorite binky immediately. As Stacey headed out the door on a cold, rainy winter night, Jude called out, "Hey, do you mind picking up a burger for me from The Grill?"

"You just ate chicken potpie," she retorted, pulling up her hood.

"I'm still hungry," he said mournfully as he walked into the den with Piper in his arms.

Stacey couldn't turn him down. He was doing her a favor by pacing with Piper, who had been crying without stop for nearly an hour. With the windshield wipers whipping from side to side, Stacey drove to the Superette, praying that she would find the treasured binky. The rain spit in her face as she rushed through the door. She studied the poor selection of binkies and chose two—just in case—then checked out.

Next stop, The Grill. She went inside and placed the take-out order. Pacing the front of the restaurant, she heard the jukebox playing one of her favorite songs in the bar and peeked inside at what the other half were doing tonight.

She caught a quick glimpse of Colton nursing a beer and froze. He must have sensed her looking at him because he glanced up, and his gaze locked with hers. Wanting to avoid him, she pulled back inside and prayed Jude's burger would be ready soon. She haunted the cash register. *"Hurry, hurry,"* she whispered under her breath.

"Hey, what are you doing out on a wicked night like tonight?" Colton asked from behind her.

Stacey took a deep breath and turned around. "I could ask the same of you."

Colton shrugged. "Cabin fever. I just needed to get away from the house. What are you doing here?"

"Piper lost her favorite binky, and I had to try to find one like it. Jude asked me to pick up a burger for him. He's pacing with Piper, so it's the least I can do, even though he's already had dinner."

"You want to come in here while you wait?"

She shook her head. "No, thanks." She glanced

at the checkout, but there was no sign of her take-out order. "Listen, I just want you to know the rumors aren't true."

He frowned at her. "What rumors?" he asked.

"About me." She swallowed over the sudden lump that formed in her throat. She thought she'd gotten control of herself during the past few days. Why had that control evaporated so quickly? "There was a rumor that the only reason I got involved with you was to get back at Joe. I just need you to know that isn't true."

He stared at her in disbelief. "Who said that?"

"Well, I heard from someone who heard from someone from someone, so I don't know. It's just important to me that you know it's not—"

She broke off as an attractive brunette approached Colton from behind and looped her arms around him. "Hey, baby, where'd you go?"

Colton glanced at the woman in surprise. "I thought you were busy with someone else."

She shook her head and nuzzled him seductively. "I was just trying to get your attention."

Colton cleared his throat and looked at Stacey. "Uh, this is Mary," he said.

"Malia," the woman corrected with an indulgent grin. "He's so cute, isn't he?"

"Uh-huh," Stacey said.

"Maria is new in town," he said, still messing up the woman's name. "I just met her tonight."

Stacey couldn't believe her eyes. "Nice to meet

you, Malia. How did you end up in Horseback Hollow?"

"I needed to get off the grid. Violent ex," she said. "This seemed like a good choice."

"I hope it will work out for you," Stacey said, and finally Jude's order was delivered to the register. She was so relieved she nearly shouted. "Oh, there's my takeout. Have a nice evening. I need to get back home." She paid her bill and ran out the door to her car.

Just as she slid onto her seat, Colton caught the door before she could close it. "Hey, that wasn't what you think it was," he said, rain pouring down over his head and jacket.

"It's okay," she forced herself to say. "There are no strings between us. You can do what you want. Malia probably doesn't have any little kids."

"That's not what's important," he said.

"I'm not so sure about that, and I can't say I blame you. If I were a man, I might not want to take on the baggage of a baby that wasn't mine. I understand, Colton. I really do," she said, although she wished things could be different.

Colton shook his head, but she couldn't handle this discussion any longer. Her sadness overwhelmed her. "I need to go," she said, and pulled her car door shut.

Colton called himself ten times a fool during the next twelve hours. He could barely sleep when he thought of the injured expression on Stacey's face. He should have stopped her. He shouldn't have let her go. He should have told her how much he'd missed her and that he wanted to work things out with her. Instead, he'd stood in the rain trying to come to grips with the ridiculous rumor she'd relayed to him.

Colton spent the day working in the barn. The sound of silence, however, echoed inside his mind. Unable to bear the scrutiny of his family, he decided to go into town again and get a burger from The Grill. He didn't know where else to go. This was yet another time when he needed his own place.

After placing his order, Colton carried his burger and fries from the grill to the bar and ordered a beer, hoping he didn't run into Mary or whatever her name was. He stared up at the basketball game playing on the television while he ate his meal.

"Long time, Colton," a voice from his past said.

Colton glanced over his shoulder to see Joe Hitchens. He blinked. "Hey, Joe, what you doing here?"

"I decided to pay a visit from Dallas," Joe said. Colton noticed Joe was a little chubbier than when he'd left Horseback Hollow all those months ago.

"You left town kinda fast," Colton said.

Joe shrugged. "It was a rough time for me."

"For you," Colton said, beginning to seethe. "What about Stacey?"

"She was early enough along that she could have taken care of the pregnancy," Joe said.

"Taken care of the pregnancy?" Colton echoed.

"That's what she did. She delivered that baby and has taken care of her with no help from you."

"I meant," Joe said, lowering his voice, "she could have gotten rid of the pregnancy."

Colton gaped at the man in disbelief. "You mean get rid of Piper?"

"Is that what she named the baby? I heard it was a girl," Joe said.

"But you never bothered to call her or offer any kind of support," Colton said. He pushed aside his food. He had lost his appetite.

"She knew I didn't want a kid. She shouldn't have gotten pregnant," Joe said.

"As if you had nothing to do with it," Colton said, growing angrier with each passing second. "You bastard," he said, standing and punching Joe in the face.

Colton's knuckles throbbed, and Joe covered his face.

"What the—" Joe said. "You know what kind of father I had. I didn't ever want to be a father after the kind of example my dad set. He was gone more than he was with my mom and me."

"That's no excuse. You're the lowest of the low," Colton said in disgust. "I don't know how you can call yourself a man. We've been friends since high school, but I don't recognize you anymore. When did you turn yourself into the kind of person you've become?"

"You must have gotten pretty close to Stacey to be so defensive," Joe said. "Did you go to bed with her?"

It was all Colton could do to keep from hitting Joe again. "Go back to Dallas," he said. "You don't belong here."

"Who do you think you are? Dating my ex? Bros don't cheat on bros. You know the guy code," Joe said.

"What guy code? You haven't been here for over a year. What rights do you have?" Colton asked.

"That baby is mine. That woman was mine," Joe said.

"*Was* is the operative term. What do you know about Piper?" Colton demanded.

Joe narrowed his eyes, then shifted from one foot to the other. "Not much."

"Why are you even here now?" Colton asked. "You haven't been here for months, not even when your baby was born."

Silence stretched between them. "Someone told me you and Stacey had gotten involved," Joe confessed.

"You would come back into town for that, to stake your claim on a woman you ran out on, but not when the baby was born?" Colton asked, shaking his head. "Are you crazy?"

"I should have known you wouldn't understand." Joe rubbed at his cheek where Colton had punched him. "So, is the baby okay?" Joe asked reluctantly.

"She's as close to perfect as a baby can get. She's gorgeous. Big green eyes and blond hair just like Stacey. She's got a kick to her personality. If she doesn't like what you're doing, she'll let you know. But she's the sweetest thing in the world when she falls asleep on your shoulder. Makes you feel as if everything in the world is the way it should be."

Joe stared at Colton. "You love her. You love *my* daughter," he accused.

Colton met Joe's astonished gaze and nodded. "Yeah. I guess I do. I really do."

Joe raked his hand through his hair and shook his head. "I don't know what to say."

"I do," Colton said. "You need to man up or shut up. If you want Stacey and your daughter back, then you need to go tell her. I think Stacey deserves better than you, but there's more involved in this situation. There's Piper," Colton said. "I'll give you twenty-four hours."

Joe stared at him, clearly affronted. "Who are you to tell me I've got twenty-four hours?"

"I'm the man who has changed your baby's diaper, rocked her to sleep and had her poop down my back," Colton said. "Have you done any of that?"

Joe looked at him in hostile silence.

"That's right. You haven't. You've got twenty-four hours. Don't mess with me, Joe. I'm disgusted with you," Colton said, and tossed some cash on the counter and walked away.

The next twenty-four hours passed by in minute-by-minute increments. Colton thought about Stacey and Piper when he drove home, when he took his evening shower, when he brushed his teeth and when he tried to go to sleep. His attempt to sleep was completely futile.

When he got up in the morning, he didn't know how he was going to get through the day, so he did it the only way he knew how. Working. He worked clear through until six that evening. As he walked toward the house, he told himself that he only had an hour and a half to go.

"Hey, sweetheart," his mom said as he walked through the door. "You want some dinner?"

"I'm not that hungry," he muttered.

"Well, you should take in a little nourishment after spending all day outside," she said. "I fixed a pot roast. I think you'll like it."

Colton didn't protest as his mother fussed over him and urged him to take a seat at the kitchen table. In this situation, it was easier to acquiesce than fight her. His mother was clearly in supernurture mode. Colton took a few bites of pot roast and potatoes.

"You must be sick," his mother said. "You're not eating."

"The pot roast is great, but I have some things on my mind, Mom," he told her.

"What?" his mother said. "What's on your mind?"

"I don't want to talk about it," he said and rose from his chair.

"Is it Stacey Fortune Jones?" she asked.

The question stopped him in his tracks. "And what if it is?"

His mother sighed. "Give her the benefit of the doubt. Her mother says she has fallen for you. But don't tell her that I told you," his mother said.

His heart swelled at the possibility that Stacey could have *fallen* for him. He wondered when that had happened. He wondered *if* it had happened. "How do you know?"

"I met up with Jeanne the other day at the post office and we got to talking." His mother broke off and pressed her lips together. "But I'm not going to say anything else. I shouldn't interfere. This is between you and Stacey."

Colton stared at his mother in disbelief. "You give advice and opinions about everything, but now you're clamming up?"

His mother lifted her finger. "Colton, don't you bait me. I'm determined to do the right thing. You and Stacey need to figure out what's best for you," she said and turned away.

Colton, watching the clock every other minute, sighed and put his plate in the fridge to eat later. "Sorry, Mom. I'm just not hungry right now. I'll eat it for lunch tomorrow." Colton grabbed his coat and headed for his truck. Eighteen minutes to go.

He drove around for ten minutes.

Colton spotted a deer crossing the road in front of him and slowed down. The driver of a semi must have panicked, though. Colton tried to swerve out of the incoming path of the truck. But he was too late. The impact jolted him. He heard the sound of glass shattering. Pain seared through him, and everything went black.

Stacey put Piper down with ease and tossed a load of laundry into the washer for lack of anything else to do. She still couldn't get over seeing that other woman pawing Colton. He had appeared surprised, but perhaps that was because he hadn't expected the woman to follow him out of the grill. Stacey suspected Malia was everything Stacey wasn't. Employed, with no baby and no stretch marks. Malia had looked like a girl ready to have a good time, and now that Stacey was a mom, she had to think twice about throwing caution to the wind for the sake of a good time. She had to think about her little Piper.

Still, the image of Colton with Malia made her so edgy she felt as if her nerve endings were being rubbed raw with a wire brush. There wasn't anything she could do about it, she told herself. The fact that Colton hadn't tried to call her in nearly two days spoke volumes.

Stacey turned the television in her bedroom on low volume in hopes of distracting herself, but the reality show just irritated her even more. She brushed her teeth and dressed for bed, praying that she would get some relief with sleep. Just as she pulled back her covers and reached to turn out her lamp, her cell phone vibrated with an incoming call.

Spotting Rachel's number on the ID, Stacey debated letting it go to voice mail. She didn't want to discuss her feelings about Colton right now, especially with his sister. Sighing, she picked up, ready to say she didn't want to talk about Colton.

"Hey, Rachel," Stacey said. "What's up?"

"Oh, Stacey, it's terrible," Rachel said, nearly sobbing. "Colton has been in a bad accident. His truck was hit by a semi. The ambulance is taking him to the Lubbock General E.R."

Stacey's heart turned cold. She tried to make sense of what Rachel had told her. The only thing she knew for certain was that Colton had been hurt. "Do you know anything about his condition? Did they tell you anything?"

"All we know is that he's unconscious, and there may be internal injuries. Mom and Dad are driving to Lubbock in their car, and I'm going in mine. Stacey, I'm scared. I'm afraid I'm going to lose my brother."

For a moment, Stacey couldn't breathe. *She* was afraid of losing Colton, too. Even if they went back to being friends, Stacey didn't want to lose Colton. Just knowing he was alive on the earth gave her a good feeling inside her. He was a wonderful man, and the thought of not being able just to see him again made her feel like crying. Anxiety coursed through her. But some part of her professional training as a nurse kicked in.

"Don't give up yet," she said. "I'm sure he's getting good care."

"Oh, Stacey, I wish you could be here," Rachel said.

"I'm on my way," Stacey promised, even if she

had to drag Piper out of bed. She wanted to be there for Colton. She wanted to be there for his family.

Stacey changed into jeans and a sweater, then awakened her mother and told her the horrible news.

"Oh, no," Jeanne said. "That's terrible. Do you have any idea if they think he'll recover? Poor Olive and Frank must be beside themselves."

"I'd like to go to Lubbock to be with them. I'll take Piper with me, but—"

Her mother shook her head. "No. Absolutely not. I'll watch over her. You go ahead, but please be careful. And call us with any news."

Stacey gave her mother a hug and grabbed a bottle of water before she pulled on her coat and left the house. Driving through the night, she thought about all the times she'd spent with Colton. An image of him playing ball as a child flashed through her head. She remembered playing tag with Rachel, him and her brothers. Later on, when they'd become teenagers and she'd passed him in the hall, he'd never been too cool to wave to her as a younger student.

Now that she knew him as a man, her feelings were even stronger. Yes, he'd become the most sexy man in existence to her, but it was partly due to his tenderness and encouragement. It was partly due to the way that he tried so hard with Piper. How could she possibly resist Colton after all that?

She made the drive in record time and pulled into the parking lot at the hospital. She rushed inside to the E.R. but didn't see any Fosters. Her stomach dipped. She prayed that the worst hadn't happened. Stacey asked the registration desk about Colton, and a few moments later, she was ushered back to a waiting room.

Rachel rose and soared into Stacey's arms. "I'm so glad you're here."

Stacey couldn't help seeing Mr. and Mrs. Foster standing beside a row of chairs. Mrs. Foster's eyes were bloodshot from tears, and Mr. Foster looked dazed and shocked. Stacey's heart went out to them.

"Any news?" she asked.

"He's being examined. They said he's still unconscious," Rachel said, sniffing.

"They're looking after him," Stacey said, but she was so scared. She just couldn't show it. She turned toward Colton's parents and embraced Mrs. Foster.

"Oh, Stacey, I just want him to be okay," Mrs. Foster said.

Stacey squeezed Colton's mother tight. She wanted Colton to be all right, too. More than anything. She took a deep breath, knowing that waiting could be the worst. "Can I get coffee for any of you?"

Rachel and her parents shook their heads, all murmuring *no.*

The vigil began.

The minutes crept by slowly, feeling like days instead of hours. Stacey tried to make small talk but gave up after a half hour had passed. All of them were worried sick. Why hadn't a doctor or nurse entered the waiting room to speak to them?

Stacey was just about to prod someone at the emergency-room desk for details when a doctor walked in, still wearing his surgical scrubs. "Mr. and Mrs. Foster?" he said. "I'm Dr. McMillan. Your son took a hard hit. He has a concussion and some bad bruises. I have to say it's a miracle that your son didn't sustain more serious injuries. We'll keep him under observation until we're sure he's out of the woods from that concussion."

"Oh, stars," Mrs. Foster said, sinking onto a chair.

Stacey's heart was hammering in her head. "How much blood has he lost? Has he been conscious at all? Is there any lung damage? What about—"

"Whoa," the doctor said. "One at a time."

Stacey forced herself to pace her questions, and the doctor answered each one.

"When can the family see him?" she asked.

He glanced at his watch. "Let's give it another few moments," he warned.

The doctor left the room, and Rachel, wiping away the tears in her eyes, grabbed Stacey. "It sounds as if he's going to be okay," she said.

Stacey wanted to see Colton and touch him, check his stats to be sure, but she nodded. "It sounds very good."

Moments later, the Fosters were led back to see Colton in recovery. Stacey paced the waiting room, praying and wishing for Colton. Ten minutes later, a nurse appeared in the doorway. "Stacey, I understand you're Colton Foster's girlfriend. The rest of the family requested your presence."

Stacey nodded and followed the nurse to the recovery room. Colton was receiving fluids and oxygen. Her heart squeezed tight in fear. At the same time, she knew these measures were medically necessary.

"Why does he have all these tubes?" Mr. Foster asked, his face filled with fear.

Rachel reached for Stacey's hand.

"All these things are helping support Colton to recover from his injuries and the accident," Stacey said. "Soon enough, he won't be needing the line for fluids. Later, they'll only give him oxygen as needed. This is the worst, except for any bruising and swelling he may have. It looks like they're taking good care of him. That's what's important."

"Stacey, I'm so glad you're here," Rachel said.

"Me, too," Olive said and grabbed Stacey's hand.

Mr. Foster took a deep breath and looked at his son.

The three of them stood in the recovery area for several moments. "Even though Colton is unconscious, he can hear your voices, so talking is good for him."

Rachel immediately went to Colton's side and started chatting. Her voice suddenly broke. "I love you, big brother. Wake up soon," she said, and kissed him gently on his forehead.

His mother took a turn next. "I'm sorry I didn't

answer your questions tonight," she said and sniffed. "I love you. Everybody loves you."

His father stepped closer. "You're a good man. A good, strong man. Get better, son. We're here for you."

Stacey's throat tightened in a knot of emotion. She hated how much all of them were hurting. She didn't want to think about her own feelings. The three of them looked at her expectantly, as if they wanted her to speak to Colton, too.

Stacey slowly walked to Colton's side and gently touched his shoulder. "Hey, you. What are you doing playing chicken with semis?" She bit her lip. "We want you to get better, but don't work too hard at it. Let the medicine help you," she said.

Colton's eyelids fluttered. He opened his mouth and coughed. "Stacey? Stacey?"

Stunned that he would call her name, she leaned closer. "I'm here. I'm here. What do you need?"

"Joe?" he said.

She frowned. "Joe?"

"Did he come see you?"

Stacey figured Colton must be talking out of his head. "No. I haven't seen Joe," she said, but Colton had fallen asleep.

Chapter Twelve

Stacey sat by Colton's side for the next several hours. She urged Mr. and Mrs. Foster to return home, but Rachel insisted on staying. Colton awakened for short periods. Sometimes he blinked his eyes. He often asked questions as to why he was in the hospital. He asked again about Joe but fell back asleep.

"Why do you think he keeps asking about Joe?" Rachel asked.

"I have no idea," Stacey said. "Joe hasn't been in town for ages."

"Maybe he has amnesia. Maybe this is part of his concussion," Rachel suggested.

"I don't know," Stacey said. "If it keeps happening, maybe we should ask the doctor about it."

Colton's parents returned and shooed both Rachel and Stacey away to take a break. Gritty-eyed and tired, but mostly confident that Colton was on the road to recovery, Stacey returned home and fell into bed. When she awakened, it was early evening, and she checked on Colton via his parents. He'd been moved to a room and was doing much better.

Stacey sighed with relief and spent the rest of the afternoon taking care of Piper. Her daughter seemed thrilled to see her, which eased some of the upset and trauma she'd experienced during the past week. Rocking Piper to sleep was the purest form of therapy for Stacey. She kissed her sweet baby's head and put her to bed. Afterward Stacey updated her mother about Colton and his injuries. Thank goodness, her mother didn't ask any probing questions about Stacey's feelings about Colton. She went to bed, planning to visit Colton the next morning.

The next morning, Stacey dressed Piper in a cute pink outfit and made the hour-long trip to Lubbock. Piper snoozed on and off, and was so quiet Stacey had to check every now and then to make sure the baby was breathing. When they arrived at the hospital, Stacey changed Piper's diaper in the backseat of the car in the parking lot. The cold winter wind whipped around her. Piper's eyes widened like saucers from the chill.

"Wheee, that's breezy, isn't it?" she said, quickly

refastening Piper's pink outfit and pulling her baby up against her.

Stacey tucked Piper under her coat as she made her way to Colton's room, where his parents sat next to him.

"Hi," she said. "I thought you might enjoy some visitors."

Colton looked up, and, seeing Piper, he gave a groggy smile. "Hey, how's the little one doing?"

"Great. She barely made a peep on the way. An hour's drive. There's hope that she will be a good traveler."

"Joe didn't come to see you, did he?" Colton asked.

Stacey slid a questioning glance toward Colton's parents, but his mother just shook her head and rose. "Come on, Frank. Let's get some coffee."

"I just had coffee," Frank said.

"Well, I want some more," Olive said firmly.

Frank sighed and rose to his feet. "Thanks for coming," he said to Stacey and gave a little wave to Piper.

"You've mentioned Joe several times," Stacey said. "I thought it was a result of your concussion. Why do you keep talking about him? Did you have a hallucination?"

Colton gave a short laugh, then grabbed his bruised ribs. "No hallucination. He showed up at the bar the other day."

Shocked and confused, Stacey stared at Colton. "Joe? In Horseback Hollow? Are you sure?"

"Yeah, I punched him in the face," Colton said.

Stacey covered her mouth with her free hand. "Oh, my goodness. How did that happen?"

"Easy," Colton said. "He opened his mouth and started talking. I gave him twenty-four hours to go see you. Then, I told him I was taking my turn."

Stacey sank onto a chair, pulling Piper onto her lap. She shook her head but felt no sadness. "He never showed."

Colton took a deep breath and winced. "The night of the wreck, I was counting down the minutes to come see you."

Stacey's heart squeezed tight. "Oh, Colton, no." She rubbed her forehead. "That means you would have never had that accident if you had decided to stay home and wait until morning."

"I couldn't wait," Colton said. He closed his eyes. "I have a confession to make. Back before Joe proposed to you, I told him he needed to put a ring on your finger. You're a special girl, and someone was going to steal you away. He proposed to you the next day." Colton sighed, opening his eyes, his gaze full of regret. "I always felt guilty—that maybe you wouldn't have gotten pregnant if I hadn't given Joe that push."

Stacey blinked at the revelation. She felt a rush of emotions. All those months ago, Colton had been protective of her. What Colton told her just confirmed what she already knew. Joe had never truly loved her. He might not have wanted to lose her, but he hadn't loved her. "I hate that he had to be pushed along, and that I believed in him. I hate that he abandoned both Piper and me. But I could never regret having Piper. She's the light of my life."

"Yeah, but that doesn't change the fact that you've been through a terrible time because of Joe."

"Why did you give him twenty-four hours?" Stacey asked.

Colton shrugged his shoulders and winced slightly. He looked away, then back at her. "I'm in love with you. I don't know exactly when it happened or how. It just did. I fell in love with you. And Piper. Maybe I shouldn't have threatened Joe—"

"Stop," she said breathlessly and nearly fell out of the chair. "Did you just say you love me?"

He narrowed his eyes. "Yeah, I did."

"And Piper. You love her, too?"

"I do," he said, almost defiantly.

Stacey jumped from her chair and planted a kiss on his mouth. "I love you, too, Colton Foster. So very, very much."

He met her gaze. "Are you sure?"

"Very, very sure. I feel like the luckiest woman in the world. Say it again, please. Say you love me again so I can be sure. I feel like I dreamed it."

"I love you, Stacey Fortune Jones. I want you to be Stacey Fortune Jones Foster," he said.

Her heart stopped in her chest. "I feel as if I'm walking in a dream."

"I want to make your dreams come true as much as I possibly can," he said. "Even if that means sitting in tiny chairs I'm afraid of breaking for the sake of having a tea party with Piper."

Stacey's eyes filled with tears. "Oh, Colton."

Piper made a chirpy sound, and he turned to her. "I wanted to take this slow and be sensible, but life is too short. Stacey and Piper, will you marry me?"

"Yes, yes and yes," Stacey said and kissed Colton again.

His parents walked into the room. "Everything okay?" Mrs. Foster asked.

"Everything's great," Colton said. "Stacey, Piper and I are getting married."

"Well, thank goodness," his mother said, her voice full of relief and emotion. "We couldn't be happier."

"I guess we're going to have to build a house on the ranch for you three," Mr. Foster said. "We'll get started as soon as possible."

"Dad, I'd really like you to see a doctor about your back. I don't want you working on a house for me when you might hurt yourself."

His father frowned and shrugged. "Your sister's taking me for an appointment to see a doctor next week. I didn't want to do it, but she told me I owed it to you. I'm gonna hire a full-time hand and a few part-time guys, too. It's time. I've got more money in the bank than anyone knows, but don't spread that around. We'll get through. I just want you to get well."

Stacey squeezed one of Colton's hands. "This means you can concentrate on getting better," she said. "That's what we all want."

The next day, Colton arrived home from the hospital and was recovering by leaps and bounds. His doctor called him superhuman because he was healing so quickly. Stacey constantly chided him to take his time and rest, but she could see he found it hard not to forge into his regular routine. She visited him every day, and every day, it seemed as if their love for each other grew stronger.

A few days after that, Colton stood with her in the den of her parents' home. The room was usually a warm, welcoming place for family and visitors, but not today.

Today, the visitor was the biological father of her child. Stacey had fought the meeting with Joe, but Colton had insisted that she and Piper deserved some support from Joe. Stacey couldn't be less interested in seeing Joe. In many ways, she didn't want Piper exposed to such a man. She could only hope that someday he would grow up.

A knock sounded at the door, and she looked at

Colton. "You'll be okay," he said. "I'm here with you. You're just looking out for Piper. Remember that."

Stacey took a deep breath and answered the door to her former fiancé and Piper's biological father. He didn't look nearly as handsome as she remembered. She wondered how that had happened. "Hi, Joe. Come on inside," she said.

Joe entered with a slightly ill expression on his face. "Yeah, uh. I know I need to give you child support," he said. "I should have done it before, but I just couldn't face the idea that I had a child. I'll catch up," he promised.

"That's good," Stacey said. She wouldn't thank him. This was long overdue. "Do you want to see her?"

Joe took a deep breath. "Yeah. Yeah. I want to see her," he said as if he were facing the guillotine.

"I'll go get her," Stacey said, and collected Piper from her mother who was staying in the kitchen. Jeanne was still too angry with Joe to face him, and Stacey had made sure her father was working away from the house that day. She picked up her precious baby girl and carried her to the front foyer.

Joe stared at Piper for a long moment. "She's beautiful."

"Yes, she is and always has been," Stacey said. "I can't thank you for how you left us, but I can thank you for giving her to me."

Joe pursed his lips together in sadness. "I'd like to try to see her every now and then."

"I think she deserves that," Stacey said. "I think she deserves the best you can give her."

Joe gave a slow nod. "I don't know how to be a good father. I never had one. I'm gonna need some hints and nudges. My father was never there for me when I needed him. I was afraid I couldn't be a good father when you told me you were pregnant. That's why I told you that you should—" He cleared his throat. "I was wrong," he said in a gruff voice.

"You can put your meetings with Piper on your schedule on your smartphone calendar. You put your other appointments on there, don't you?" Colton asked.

"Yeah. I never thought of that," Joe said.

"You can start now, then," Colton said. "Input a date three weeks from today to call Stacey about when you can see Piper."

Joe pulled his cell phone from his pocket and tapped the information into his calendar. "Done. I'm sorry for the pain I've caused you, Stacey. But I'm going to try and—" Joe glanced at Colton. "It looks like you're in good hands now."

Stacey smiled. "Best hands ever," she said.

Ten days later, Rachel insisted on taking care of Piper for a full twenty-four-hour time period. Colton had completely recovered from the accident. He picked up Stacey and drove his new truck to Vicker's Corners so they could take a stroll downtown and spend the night at a bed-and-breakfast after dinner.

"It's perfect, but freezing," Stacey said, snuggling her gloved hands in his.

"It's the dead of winter," he said and looked down at her. "But I'm glad you think it's perfect."

"If I'm with you, it's perfect," she said. "And if you're recovering—"

"Mostly there," he said.

"But don't push it," she urged. "If you're recovering, that's perfect, too. Things could have been terribly different." Her heart caught at the thought of losing Colton, and her smile fell.

Colton caught her chin with his thumb. "Hey, no sad faces tonight. We're together and happy, right?"

Stacey nodded. "Yes, yes, yes."

"I like the sound of that word," he said with a sly, sexy look. "Let's have dinner," he said, and they stepped inside the restaurant.

The host led them to a table in front of a fireplace. "Oh, this is fabulous. I feel as if I'm in heaven."

"It gets better," he promised.

They ordered dinner and were served a delicious meal. Stacey savored every bite. She patted her belly toward the end of the dinner. "I don't think I can eat any more, but I would love some of that chocolate dessert."

"I'll get it to go," he said.

After he paid the check, they walked to their charming suite at the bed-and-breakfast. Stacey couldn't remember a more wonderful evening. With Piper in Rachel's care, and the full support of her family and Colton's, she couldn't feel happier to have such a special evening with Colton. A bottle of champagne welcomed them as they walked into the room. A gas fire flickered in the fireplace.

"Like it?" he asked.

"Oh, it's amazing," she said. "I love a gas fireplace. No work and all the pleasure."

"Does that mean you'd like that in my house plans?" he asked.

"I don't need a gas fireplace to be happy with you," she insisted.

"I've got a lot packed into my savings account, Stacey. Speak up about what you want," he said, putting his arm around her back.

"Okay," she whispered. "Gas fireplace and hot tub big enough for you and me."

Colton's eyes darkened with sensuality. "Sold. I like the way you think," he said, and took her mouth in a kiss.

With Colton holding her in his arms, she almost forgot about her surroundings. It was so good to hold him and kiss him. It was so good to be alone with him and to know he was healed from the accident.

Colton pulled back. "Let's have a glass of champagne," he said.

Stacey would rather have had a bucketful of Colton, but she went along with him. He pulled the champagne bottle from the ice and popped the cork. Grabbing a glass, he spilled the bubbly liquid into the flute and offered it to her. He poured a second flute for himself.

"To you," he said. "The woman I love. I've asked you once, but I want to do it the right way this time."

Colton knelt on one knee, and Stacey's breath hung in her throat. The past few weeks had caused such a roller coaster of emotions. She felt as if she were taking another heart-pounding turn on the ride. "What are you doing?"

He pulled a jeweler's box from his pants pocket and flipped it open to reveal a beautiful diamond ring. "Will you marry me?"

Stacey's heart squeezed so tight she could hardly speak. "Oh, yes, Colton. I can't believe how lucky I am."

Colton rose to his feet and kissed her again. "I feel the same way, Stacey Fortune Jones. I can't wait for you, Piper and me to start our lives together."

Stacey couldn't believe how her life had turned out. She was in love with the best man ever, and her daughter would have a daddy to show her the stuff of which a real man was made.

Stacey had never believed much in chance, but

she'd just received the best fortune ever in Colton Foster. Love forever. She'd come from a long line of lovers, and now she was getting her chance at the love of a lifetime.

* * * * *

Don't miss the next installment in the new Special Edition continuity,
THE FORTUNES OF TEXAS: WELCOME TO HORSEBACK HOLLOW!

Can bachelor-with-a-heart-of-gold Jude Fortune Jones offer beautiful Gabriella Mendoza a chance at the love she's always wanted?

Look for
A SWEETHEART FOR JUDE FORTUNE
by Cindy Kirk
On sale February 2014, wherever Harlequin books are sold.

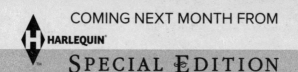

REQUEST YOUR FREE BOOKS!

2 FREE NOVELS PLUS 2 FREE GIFTS!

⟡ HARLEQUIN®

SPECIAL EDITION

Life, Love & Family

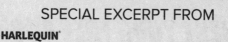
***

"You've got more experience to put on your resume now. If you really want to leave, do it."

She made a soft sound. "Probably not the best time for job hopping."

"Being pregnant, you mean." His soft words brushed against her temple and his thighs moved slowly against hers.

She exhaled shakily. "Mmm-hmm."

"You wouldn't have to work at all if you didn't want to."

She shook her head, though rubbing her cheek against the warmth radiating from him was probably the real motive. She forced herself to stop. To lift her head so there was at least one part of her not plastered against him.

She realized he'd danced her farther away from the others than she realized. "I'm not going to be your kept woman, Pax, if that's where you're heading."

His head lowered and she felt his lips against her cheek. "Baby mama doesn't fly for you?"

She slowly shook her head.

"What about wife?"

Something inside her chest fisted.

Beatrice had warned her he'd head that direction.

She pulled back again as far as his arm surrounding her would allow, which wasn't far. "Getting married just because I'm pregnant is a bad idea. We already agreed."

"I didn't agree," he said quietly. "I just didn't choose to debate the issue with you."

She didn't know why she was tearful all of a sudden. Only that she was, and there was no way he could fail to notice. "Please don't do this here," she whispered thickly.

He lifted one hand, touching her cheek gently. "Shea."

Tenderness from him would be her undoing. "You're supposed to be celebrating your best friend's wedding," she reminded.

"I'm celebrating my best friend's *marriage*. Anyone can have a wedding. Erik and Rory are going to have something a lot more important. Something that lasts a lifetime."

"And maybe they'll get there," she conceded huskily. "Right now they love each other, at least. They're starting out with a better reason than pregnancy."

His feet stopped moving altogether, though he still held her close. "Why is it so hard for you to see what's right in front of your face?"

Her throat felt like a vise was tightening around it. "I don't want us to end up hating each other."

Despite the dim lighting, his eyes searched hers, leaving her feeling raw. Exposed.

"There's no rule that says we will."

***

Enjoy this sneak peek from
USA TODAY *bestselling author Allison Leigh's*
ONCE UPON A VALENTINE, the latest book in
THE HUNT FOR CINDERELLA *miniseries.*